Nature Visions

SHADOW HAMILTON

authorHOUSE

AuthorHouse™ UK
1663 Liberty Drive
Bloomington, IN 47403 USA
www.authorhouse.co.uk
Phone: UK TFN: 0800 0148641 (Toll Free inside the UK)
UK Local: (02) 0369 56322 (+44 20 3695 6322 from outside the UK)

© 2024 Shadow Hamilton. All rights reserved.

No part of this book may be reproduced, stored in a retrieval system, or transmitted by any means without the written permission of the author.

Published by AuthorHouse 07/12/2024

ISBN: 979-8-8230-8867-1 (sc)
ISBN: 979-8-8230-8868-8 (e)

Library of Congress Control Number: 2024914485

Print information available on the last page.

Any people depicted in stock imagery provided by Getty Images are models, and such images are being used for illustrative purposes only.
Certain stock imagery © Getty Images.

This book is printed on acid-free paper.

Because of the dynamic nature of the Internet, any web addresses or links contained in this book may have changed since publication and may no longer be valid. The views expressed in this work are solely those of the author and do not necessarily reflect the views of the publisher, and the publisher hereby disclaims any responsibility for them.

Contents

My Sun 1
Night 2
Snow 3
An Eagle 4
Softly 5
Night Shadows 6
Carnal Feelings 7
Jack the Lad 8
Flowering 9
Owl Etheree 10
Dusk Falls Softly 11
Changes 12
Meat 13
Butterflies 14
Silence 15
They Call It Sport 16
Nature 17
Heading North 18
A Woman Scorned 19
The Moon and the Stars 20
The Druid 21
Witches and Warlocks 23
Fish 24
The Ruin 25
The Child 27
Burnished Skies 28
Through Your Eyes 29
The Rut 30
Sweet Music 31
Night Sky 32
Lifting Veils 33
The Ride of a Life Time 34
Visions In the Mist 35

Daydream 36
Willow 37
Rodeo 38
Morning Mist 39
The Quiet Beat 40
Blossoms and Bubbles 41
Sailing 42
Spring Beckons 43
They Call 44
Yet Again 45
Awash With Colour 46
Hush 47
Rain Soaked Land 48
Equinox 49
Magnet 50
Oops I Slipped Up 51
A Tribal War 52
The Ostrich 53
Winter's End 54
Nightingale 55
Time Warp 56
Circles 57
Spring Dreams 58
Moon Rays 59
From Sky 60
Nativity 61
Memoirs 62
Winter Solstice 64
Nice Things 65
A Hush 66
The Old Year 67
Festivity 68
I Dream 69
Spare a Thought 70
Jack Frost 71
Santa 72

Victims	73
Atstan Impresario	74
No Shame Or Blame	76
Winds of the World	77
Darkness	78
Autumn Oak Tree	79
Friendship	80
Loneliness	81
A Mote of Dust	82
Him	83
Winter Days	84
Dank Pants	85
A Turning Point	86
Chopped 11	87
I Am	88
Flashing Eyes	89
Day Break	90
Yesterday's Joys	91
Near Death Experience	92
Take Over	93
Savannah Night	95
Day To Night and Back	96
Faith Healer	97
Chill Night	98
My Owner	99
Cowboys In the Badlands	100
In the Desert	101
Death Calls	102
Zincograph Plate	103
Shades of Autumn	104
The End Is Nigh	105
A Thing Called Love	106
In Love's Shadow	107
Under the Surface	108
Remnants of Love	109
A Naked Beauty	110

Through the Mist	111
Piano Visions	112
Skirl of the Piper	113
Wanderer	114
Exquisitely Enchanting	115
Fishy Tale	116
Relentless Time	117
Danger Lurks	118
Animals Alive	119
Silver Beams	120
Reaffirmed	121
Carelessness	122
How Doth	124
Goethe's Path	125
Outback Truckers	126
Past Lives	128
Uncle Roy	129
Noble Beasts	130
I Did It My Way	132
Lonely Cloud	133
All About Leadership	134
Moonlight Passion	135
Elephant Rage. A True Story	136
School Gate	138
Day the Earth Reversed	140
Swimming With Dolphins	141
In the Gloaming	142
Ode To My Hills	143
Moon Ode	144
As Darkness Descends	145
The Darkness At Noon	146
Silent Killer	147
Gender Bender	148
Viking Plunder	149
Old Loves	150
Flower Garden	151

Secrets	152
A Daydream	153
For the Love Of	154
Do You Really Know Him	156
A Broken Heart	159
Ghost Rider	160
Lost	161
The Drifter	162
The Stones	163
Life's Mountain	164
Hitching a Ride	165
A Ring of Stones	166
An Ode For Zante	167
Fisherman	169
Poets of Yore	170
The Magical Forest	171

My Sun

When the sun is shining its bright rays,
so too I feel its warmth heating me.
As the sun enwraps me close,
once more I blossom as it kisses me.
I feel it flooding within me
filling up each and every crevasse.
Days ago I still lived in darkness
hidden and locked away.
Now I gladly step up to your sun
which has brought me back.
Dark so sober now has no fear
as I lay basking in your arms.
You came into my life softly
together we have grown
completing what was missing
Making Us as One against All.
Love crept in, neither of us
were yet aware of the future.
That a bolt of lightning
would strike us both.
Sending us rushing
head long in love.
Now the future is ours
with love we storm the world.
May your sun always be by my side
as together we journey on.
Let us share our love with all
so, they can bask in love's warmth.
Come my darling into my arms
hold me oh so very close.
I am your lady you are my man
from now to eternity, we are bound.

Shadow Hamilton

Night

The still night seemed to amplify each sound
until each soft noise vibrated loudly.
The torrid air mystic as it hovers bound
above the lake and leaping perch gleam ghostly.
A night of light mist that distorts shapes
tricking the eye as I pass on my way.
Daggling leaves and branches like grapes
brush my skin leaving a smell of hay.
Now it darkens, clouds cover the moon
the wind whips up sending all flurrying.
In this wild tempest I find a boon
that is filled brim full of loving.
The terrors of the night fade
blinded by the blazing rays,
old fears, to them bye I bade
time to welcome back love filled days.

Snow

Furiously the flakes fell, thickly coating
all they touched, breaking branches
with their weight. Yet still relentlessly
the snow cascaded seemingly ever thicker.
Freezing temperatures with icy fingers that
turned all they touched into frozen statues.
Ponds with ice two feet thick encouraging
the skaters to swirl, twirl and circle freely.
Flurry huge flakes that formed deep drifts
some topping out at fifteen feet barriers.
Suffocating sheep and many others
with its cold relentless arms of purpose.
For now, Winter reins in supremacy
killing of the weak sending some
into hibernation seeking relief
from the biting bitter cold.
Furnaces blaze and their flames dance
throwing out some warmth and comfort,
bringing a reminder that soon
Spring will once more walk our lands.

Shadow Hamilton

An Eagle

high the eagle perches
feathers that gleam in sunlight
majestic wingspan

Softly

Just like dark slowly cloaking the land
love slips in softly unfolding like a bud.
Once in a heart it expands filling it full
re-awaking those long-forgotten emotions.
Tinting all in glorious technic colours
casting a warm glow that courses
though the veins pulsing strongly
bringing vitality and sense of eagerness.
Touching all those who cross its path
spreading peace and contentment.
Bask in its light and give it full rein
and enjoy all that comes in its wake.

Shadow Hamilton

Night Shadows

Shadows flit across the valley shading
more and more they are pervading.
Changing the shapes of all they touch
of the big trees standing tall in a clutch.
Creeping along altering as it grows
here a scary monster lurks and bows,
as branches bend in the gentle wind.
Out into the clearing slips the hind.
Its size blurred in the dark gloom
and startling at the water spume
As it soars up briefly from the stream
churning the water high lighting the beam.
As dawn high lights the sky, they fade
returning to normal, to dark farewell they bade.
Mysteries of night now sleep til dark returns
resting hiding under the lush green ferns.

Carnal Feelings

My carnal feelings fly sky high
as you walk towards me smiling
turned on I let out a sigh.
Fingers trace down towards my thigh
setting my insides quivering
my carnal feelings fly sky high.
I blush and squirm going all shy
the warm flush setting loose feelings
turned on, I let out a sigh.
I wilt in your arms ending nigh
as our passions mix exploding
my carnal feelings run high.
Emotions running hot and high
course through veins like streaked lightning
turned on, I let out a sigh.
Slowly the world stops revolving
tensions freed both now quivering
my carnal feelings run high
turned on, I let out a sigh.

Shadow Hamilton

Jack the Lad

His mother told him, watch out
many a lass you will meet
with some you will dally
share a kiss or two,
some you will bed
but take care, for a lass
that's too easy is not to be wed
this advice he took to heart
with many a lass he dallied
most to his bed he took
'til one day he fell in love
with a lass called Jill
on bended knee he asked her
will you please wed me
oh no she said no never
my mother warned me of studs like you
she told me, bed them, don't wed them
for a stud he will always be

Nature Visions

Flowering

Like a bud slowly opening its petals
one by one to the sun's warmth.
So too does love creep into hearts,
once there it soon expands blossoming.
Spreading like wildfire it floods and fills
every little corner and all the cracks.
New love needs special nurturing
just like the buds. In caring hands
it thrives and grows casting all in
golden warmth that shines richly.
Releasing peace and touching
the souls of all who feel it.

Shadow Hamilton

Owl Etheree

A
Barn Owl
sits up high,
head twisting round.
Rustling undergrowth,
he swoops silently down.
Shrill screech of terror and pain,
the evil deed done, he returns home.
Three fluffy chicks hungrily await,
they feast, stocking up for the winter months.

written 09/20/2015

Dusk Falls Softly

Dusk slowly falls across the land
spooky shadows begin appearing.
Trees sway seeming to walk
waving their branches in time.
Hoots of owls on the prowl
carry far into the night.
Ghostly figures slip by
some, creatures of the night.
Others look much more sinister
yet soon fade out of sight.
Deer stealthy go to drink
and the pale moon mirrors them.
Their eyes shining bright
in the reflective light.
The night darkens
and the moon beams down.
Stars caught dance in her light
as peace covers the land.
Slowly the mystic of night passes
and dawn creeps across the sky.

Shadow Hamilton

Changes

Summer has past through
its hot sultry days of sun
Now slowly the leaves turn
glistening in hues of brown.
The air sharpens and cools
as the nights draw in faster.
Grains glimmer ready now
for plucking from their ears.
Rich scents of sun ripened fruit
hangs in the still air enticingly.
The smells of lunch mingling
to the heavily scented bouquet.
Icy fingers of winter awake
impatient to do their worst.
Soon the lands will lie
under a blanket of snow.

Meat

Anchored by its feet hangs the carcass
Butcher removes brisket and strings it
Chuck steak diced for stews and pies
Dark well matured silverside rests
Entrails give the dogs a royal feast
Flank minced for spaghetti Bolognese
Gullet chopped into stock pot simmers
Hanging meat swings as the butcher works
Icy still from the blast chiller
Juicy steaks thickly cut are parcelled up
Kebabs skewered, placed on display
Loin of beef neatly lined up
Minced steak patties for burgers
Neck used in both stock pot and stew
Offal set aside for pate and pies
Perfectly roasted beef ready to carve
Quick flash fry of rib eye seals in juices
Rump not too trimmed dribbles on grill
Sirloin anointed by a king sizzling
Tongue gently braised in gravy or stock
Utensils casting shadows on the wall
Venison from red deer's makes tasty things
Wing rib rubbed with hot spices waits
Xhosa cattle graze in pastures green
Yellowed meats set aside for soup
Zibeline hides scrapped and cured, nailed up

8/27/2015

Shadow Hamilton

Butterflies

In summer my garden comes alive
as graceful butterflies make it home.
Peacocks with vivid colours flit
from blossom to blossom
Busily working gathering nectar
pollinating as they go on to next
flower. All so pretty I love them all
visiting my climbing rambling roses.
Red Admirals, Swallow tails and monarchs
adding swathes of brilliant colour
chased by Skippers and Orange tips
as each one vies for one more bloom.
While Gatekeepers and Clouded Yellows
delicately sip from my hibiscus.
A cloud of Fritillary's descend on stocks
and Painted Ladies mock the sweet peas.
A drone of bumble bees sets the tune
for Tortoiseshells to dance to.
Purple Emperors set the scene
as they visit my asters and begonia's.
Ah! sweet summer flowers, all
are kissed by Comma's and Coppers
bringing my garden to life
with joy as they all busily work

written 08/12/2015

Silence

It whispers to me day and night
calling my name is hushed tones.
When out in company I hear it still
always there, silence patiently waits.
Walking along by my side
noticing each time I pause.
At night sat alone, telly playing
silence surrounds me, all else shut out.
Pouring in, trying to invade my soul
slowly sucking the life out of me.
Until I become an empty vessel
as brittle as dead flowers.
I try to reach up above it
but a losing battle I fight.
It permeates my being
with its insidious ways.
Now I accept it like a lover
holding silence oh so close.
Letting it in, accepting it
taking comfort in its grasp.
And as the silence plays on
I lay down in its folds.
It is now my own shadow
following wherever I go.

Written 08/09/2015

Shadow Hamilton

They Call It Sport

Trackers follow the animals,
herd them towards the waiting guns.
Big money paid by lazy hunters
who just want some trophies.
Not for them the slog through bush
they want an easy kill.
A bit or two taken to hang on walls
meat left where they fell.
Uncaring if they are endangered
they drink their beers in the hides.
Not wanting to get dirty or sweaty
they picnic on delicacies and wine.
Bodies of the slain beasts pile up
to be dragged away by scavengers.
While the men toast each other
proud of the day's work.
Tomorrow it will all be repeated
who I ask are the real beasts here?

Nature

Nature is so fantastic as she produces
gems that delight ones very soul.
She works hard behind the scenes
quietly repairing the damage we do.
I take pleasure in small little things
like butterflies flitting around flowers.
Stirring leaves to see a host of insects
that quickly scurry back into hiding.
The gorgeous colours on her palette
that tease and seduce the senses.
The stately magnificent of trees
that gently shade tender shoots.
Soaring mountains that enchant
with their sense of mystery.
Oceans that teem with life
the majesty of whales leaping.
There is so much to beguile
so many new things springing
to life, that tempt a weary soul
and put back a sense of purpose.
Nature is so very special
as she tends to the seasons.
Filling us with joy of life
and making our world special.

Shadow Hamilton

Heading North

Off into the deepest North
At the pole an arrow points.
Santa's village this way it says.
Tiny figures franticly bustling'
Only five months left
and mountains of presents
still to be made and wrapped
then loaded onto Santa's sleigh.
All the children dreaming blissfully
seeing that red nose sparkling
and hearing the whoosh
watch Santa looping the sky.
Scattering snowflakes
far and wide in his wake.
The moon beams down
and the north star twinkles.

A Woman Scorned

Later she would look back and see
the cracks that were now obvious.
How blind she once had been
in the throngs of her passion.
Twenty years of his affairs
his lies, and his betrayal.
Yet it was only by chance
that she had found out.
Out for lunch one day
she saw him at the back,
with a lovely young woman.
He was engrossed in her.
Their body language intense
she could see the hot flames.
Following when they left
she saw them enter the hotel.
Sicken to her very core
she went home and paced.
Then set his clothes on fire
gleefully watching them burn.
When he saw the flames
he knew the game was up.
He raced to try to save things
Yelling out you crazy bitch.
Then a loud screech of tires
he drove off rubber burning.
As for her, the flush of triumph
soon faded leaving her drained.
The divorce was acrimonious
the final judgement in her favour.
He now learned the hard lesson
never cross or scorn a woman.

Shadow Hamilton

The Moon and the Stars

The stars were twinkling
as the moon danced
sending beaming rays
to float over the earth.
Casting shadows over all
in the still of the night.
We lay entwined
fingers wandering southwards.
Our breath hot and passionate
as we danced the age old dance.
Reaffirming our love as
slowly we rose to climax.
By the river reflecting
the majesty of the sky.
Adding poignancy
to our deep abiding love

Nature Visions

The Druid

Far away deep in the forest there lived a druid
It was a long journey of three to four days of
hard going with no real path to speak of.
Just little trails wandering through the trees
and up hills, then plunging down into hidden valleys.
Crimson Fire lived up a mountain on a plateau in
an earth house loving built by his hands and shared
with the animals and birds of the forest and mountains
Crimson Fire had never married nor had children
his human friends were few although travellers
were made welcome as long as they were not hunters.
He lived as one with nature reaping her crops
abiding by the natural rules and never taking life.
A powerful high priest that used his magic for good
he shunned the ways of town and city folk.
One day a teenager approached his abode
a strapping lad sent by his father to study
and learn the druid ways. Crimson Fire
looked him up and down and thought
to himself that Young Sam would do.
"Greetings" said Sam, "from my father
Blue Dragon" Polite too thought Crimson Fire
as he returned the greetings. "I will be setting
you some tasks that will show the path to your
Future. The first is one of mediation which
you will do further up the mountain. Seek
out the cave on the next plateau and light
the fire, when it is glowing sprinkle on these
herbs and they will clear your mind and cleanse
your spirit." Sam made his way up to the cave
and followed Crimson Fire's instructions and
slipped into a deep trance as he inhaled the
smoke. Strange images danced before his eyes

not to be shared with us mere mortals.
In two days time he returned to Crimson Fire's
abode and sat with him relating all that he had
experienced. The old Druid nodded his head
wisely and asked what the last vision was?
Sam said it was an eagle that was covered in
flames. "That will be your Druid name Fire Eagle
In three days time at the summer solstice I as
high priest will call you into the druid circle
and perform the naming ceremony but first
you must go out into the forest to the east.
When you reach the tumbling rock your next
task will become clear" So Sam set off again.
Travelling far to the east he came up on the
tumbling rock. Trapped fast by its leg was
a young fawn, its mother circling nervously
both crying to the other. Sam gently approached
and slowly and carefully removed some rocks
freeing the fawn who quickly darted to his mother.
She fixed Sam with a stare then nodded her head.
Together they slipped off between the trees.
Sam set off once more heading westwards now
The skies opened and rain lashed down soaking all
and the rolling thunderclaps grew louder and louder
and lightning flashed in streaks across the sky.
An ancient oak highlighted showed a bird dashed
to the ground sodden feathers preventing it from
flying making is easy prey for the wolves, Sam
frightened them off with his staff and collected up
the bird. You need some healing he thought more
than I can give you and he carried the raven to
Crimson Fire. "You have done well young Sam, rest
now, tomorrow is the time of the solstice."
to be continued…

written 07/10/2015

Witches and Warlocks

Strong the witches circle,
around the fire, they are
dancing in ecstasy,
chanting to summon him
the powerful warlock

07/08/2015

Shadow Hamilton

Fish

flashes of silver
as they leap the waterfall
on their way to spawn

Nature Visions

The Ruin

It stood on the top of the hill
dominating all of its surrounds.
Its drawbridge these days lay open
spanning with ease the now dry moat.
Like a fairy tale fortress it had turrets
that soared up high brushing the clouds.
Its four towers majestic as blankly,
they stared, covering all points of the compass.
Slit windows peered out of casements
through walls up to six feet thick.
The massive double oak doors
fifteen feet high and twelve wide
stood thrown open allowing glimpses
of the enormous courtyard beyond.
Battlements led to each round tower
that once housed the nobles.
Old battered forgotten furniture
grandly carved four poster beds.
A sword or two lay scattered
amidst the clutter and bird dropping.
Wide stone staircases meandered
curling round and round the walls.
A gallery or two dotted here and there
perfect hiding places above the hall.
Some for musicians to play unseen
Their notes floating through the air
as below the dancers swept and strutted
as the ladies hooped dresses swirled.
Long tables once laden with food
stood a skiff with broken legs.
Wooden pint tankards higgledy piggledy
strewn about midst wooden platters.
Tattered standards limply lay motionless

Shadow Hamilton

against walls dotted with scattered torches.
The Lord of these lands killed in distant lands
leaving an infant son removed to the city
by his grieving mother who sought to forget.
Now ninety years later his grandson views
the devastation of years of neglect and vows
to return the castle to the glory of its heydays.
After three long years of often brutal work
removing shrubbery, moss and decay
Life starts to re-emerge Flags flutter
gaily high up on the battlements.
Chandeliers sparkle and the torches flicker
Tables once more groan with a feast of food
Happy shrieks of laughter fill the grand hall
And one would swear the castle wore a smile,
as children played around the buttresses.

Nature Visions

The Child

The child sits in the sun-drenched meadow
appearing to stare very intensely afar,
what captures the child's interest?
Nothing that is obvious to any of us.
He seems to be listening intently
is it to the robin who is singing?
The wind brushes across his skin
and he shivers as it touches him.
His mother quietly approaches
gently takes his hand in hers.
He clings tightly and nuzzles her
drawing in her scent to his nostrils.
The sad truth is that this child
is both deaf and blind
no sounds he hears
and no pictures he sees.
He is trapped in a silent world.
And will never see his mother's face.
yet he recognizes her scent
he feels the wind on his skin.

Shadow Hamilton

Burnished Skies

Cloaking a Burnished Coppery Sky
the darkness fully ebony black
hides the blaze of silvery stars.
Not a single twinkle could be seen.
Then like a true goddess of light
she rode out of the darkest black
and her silvery beams conquered
sending packing that bleak dark.
Now released streaks of copper
heighted and high lit her beams.
Triumphant riding the starry night
the Moon shone out in Full Glory.

Through Your Eyes

Her eyes were him wanting
as she sat waiting
dark secrets she hid
teasing glances bid
him come to her side
there to always abide

written 06/12/2015

Shadow Hamilton

The Rut

Late September the hills ring with bellows
as stags roar their challenges with gusto
collecting up the does into large herds
ready to give battle to the very death.
Walkers be wary as you too are an intruder
many have been pierced by their sharp antlers
The nine pointers in his full prime paws in anger
this is his land he is master of all he peruses.
No tolerance for the young contender
they briefly spar and the youngster flees
it is not yet his time maybe in a year or two.
The master stag bellows out his triumph.
A rustle in the undergrowth, and a loud crash
heralds the arrival of another stag in his prime
they meet with a ground shaking crash of antlers
locked in mortal combat they fight for hours.
The ground ripped up and red with their blood
they struggled back and forth, neither yielding
The challenger now weakened gives ground
as with a final clash he turns and limps off.
The master roars out his victory of this day,
gathering up his does takes them to water.
It will be his sperm this year that is carried on
His fawns that will rollick and frolic the meadows

Sweet Music

When you hear the gentle notes that seduce
or the crashing chords that vibrate
leaving your hairs standing on end
and goose bumps adorn your skin.
The sweet melody of a mouth organ
mingling with sharp piano notes.
The screeching notes of violins
harmonising with the wind pipes.
The tenderness that entices
and enhances as a fiddlers
fingers and bow fly entrancingly
all coming together as a whole.
The husky croon of a singer
melding with spine thrilling chords.
This and oh so very much more
is the sheer enchanting perfection.
Surely music is indeed soul food
the bass guitar throbbing
deep inside, whilst heaven wards
the rumbling rhythm soars.

Shadow Hamilton

Night Sky

I came out of the supermarket to be greeted
by the most amazing sky so stunning I stopped
and just stared navy blue background lined
by startling sapphire streaks that were layered.
Isles of azure blue all around were dotted
and the Clifton suspension bridge framed
perfectly as if an artist had just painted
it amidst the towers that above it soared.
Driving along admittedly gawking nearly crashed
fast as possible I got to a clear spot and stared
got out heart thumping in pure joy totally bedazzled
by the superb spectacle of various blues intermingled.
As full dark came away it all faded
I rushed home and a pen I grabbed
yet I knew that justice beyond me laid
it would take a master for it to be captured

Lifting Veils

In the dead of night veils uplift on Mid Summer's Eve,
still a time for a few live sacrifices, so tread warily.
A time when briefly the gates of hell can open
and unworldly things spew forth intent on evil.
Mid-Summer Night dreams can come to pass
most oft to those who's hearts are true and pure.
A night of extremes, of evil versus good, and
of the fires of covens and black magic.
A night where Pan himself comes forth
playing his Pipes with gleeful skirls.
Tempting and enticing the unwary souls
with false promises and exciting dreams.
Goddesses of Light dance around in circles
their task to push back the evils of hell
to allow departed lovers to hold their beloved
for a fleeting moment to love once more.

Shadow Hamilton

The Ride of a Life Time

Free wheeling down the hill
chuck-a-bang out of fuel
referring quickly to my map
a gas pump is what I need.
Right at the bottom of the hill
appears a grand and wacky
garage flying a flag and a sign
fill up here folks your last chance.
Barely making it I pull in
and soon the gas chugs
happily filling up my tank
getting high on the fumes.
Sign says open on café door
I fight my way through
the muddy forecourt
to the ramshackle hut.
Filling up on eggs and grits
total cost comes to ten bucks
walking out I get back on
backfiring like a ray-gun.
I ride off down the block
bravo someone hollers
as with clatter and bang
I follow on down the route
Oh yah freedom ahead
as my bike revs loudly
I chug-a-chug down
the famous route 66.
Old signs a-plenty
diners right out
of the fifty's line
good ole route 66

Visions In the Mist

As dawn breaks across the rugged land,
vague shapes begin to blurrily appear.
images of mythical creatures now seen
briefly then brushed away they dissolve.
Is it these images that give legends birth?
the tales of Unicorns and dragons?
The stories of three headed beasts
that wander through the mist shrouds?
Pea soup mists that you can almost push aside
abruptly vanishing as the sun burns them off.
Leaving the landscape we all know and accept
yet memories remain of fantastical things.
That re-emerge in our dreams
leaving us with uncertainty and
knowledge deep down within
that mist cloaks and blinds
what lies beyond the veils of time

Shadow Hamilton

Daydream

She rolled down her silky sheer stockings
gives him a saucy sexy look,
imaging his hands there instead
gently coursing her trim figure.
Feels his eyes following his hands,
as she submits to her passion.
wishing that he could lay with her
as they transcended to heaven.
Alas it could never be, for he,
was only a marble statue.
Crafted by her, in memory
of the hours they once had shared

Willow

The ancient brave weeping willows
that line the gentle river banks
cry not, one single drop hovers.
It is wisdom that drips from it.
This wisdom garnered through ages
of watching antics and follies
of mankind repeating same mistakes.
So they drip their wisdom in hope.
Hope is inspired by these trees
as majestically they stand.
Lines marching along river bank
they are sentinels of wisdom.

Shadow Hamilton

Rodeo

It was a hot and dusty day
the crowd fidgets as it waits
bull dripping sweat in shute bay.
howdy folks the announcers say
Raging Tornado in Shute awaits
it was a hot and dusty day.
Saddle slipping this and that way
only held in place by weights
bull dripping sweat in shute bay.
R.T. chews on his cud of hay
pawing the ground in anger waits
it was a hot and dusty day.
Flies out of Shute now comes what may
saddle slips man evacuates
bull dripping sweat in Shute bay.
Riders distract bull hold at bay
while man slides out and valuates
It was a hot and dusty day
bull dripping sweat in Shute bay.

Morning Mist

The mist swirls through the deep vale
shifting slowly and giving glimpses
of the lush vegetation and flowers.
Slowly it dissipates in dawn's sunlight.
Teasing as it lazily drifts
showing for a brief second
a colourful bank rife with flowers.
Then blankets it from sight.
As the day warms up
it appears to thicken
then yield oh so slowly.
Wisps of mist now fading.
Before our eyes lies
startling beauty.
Nature's riches displayed
a wealth of orange and yellow.
Pinks, purples and blues vie
each more beautiful
and lavish green trees
gently shade the saplings.
The Treasure of Nature's Canvas
is now stretched out before us
while the birds happily sing
as they rush to build their nests.
Insects buzz with joy as they collect
the pollen and nectar from flowers.
In this new spring day
life itself is reaffirmed.

Shadow Hamilton

The Quiet Beat

Listen to the beat of life, hear its thunder,
yet underneath lurks a murmuring whisper.
Some days almost unheard, others louder
always there it taunts, teasing like a lover.
Deep within you know who makes this whisper,
it is life itself ticking away as you falter.
Yes now it shows its face as it comes closer,
our old friend death claims us with loud clamour.

Nature Visions

Blossoms and Bubbles

As I entered the garden the scents enticed
rampant rose blossom the arches fenced.
Cascading aromatic blossoms greeting me
amidst the climbers were the sweet pea.
In the centre stood the patio so glamorous
sparkling bubbles of champagne so amorous.
Tickling the throat buds saturated with scent
from the tumbling blossoms as they descent.
Blood stream and breath full of roiling bubbles
and past swish the gentry parading in couples.
Raise your glasses in a toast as friends are wed
laughing, knowing they will all too soon be in bed.
Ah what a perfect day in this romantic garden
bubbles and blossoms tumbling as skies darken
Blossoms and bubbles never somniferous
Mixed together they are becoming toxiferous.

written 25 March 2015

Shadow Hamilton

Sailing

The sails snapped in the wind as the yacht changed tack
soon to refill as the yacht skimmed over the sea racing onwards
riding the large waves with adapt a plume slicing them apart.
Dolphins playfully following as they leapt for pure joy
spinning several times before diving down deep.
Ganging up on a lurking shark they soon send it away.
The screech of pulleys as we prepare to tack once more
as the boom crashes past to be brought up sharp
when it takes all of the free lines and sails puff up.
The ocean is sparkling in the sunlight with white crested waves
as we round the headland and now can sail with the wind
the yacht leaning far over as her gib sail speeds her on.
Now it is time to add more canvas as we flash by
the winning line now in sight and with a great cheer
from the yacht club Casaroba crosses the line in first.

Spring Beckons

With a small puff the breeze lazily blew the clouds
slowly they began to scatter and then reformed.
Steadily the wind increased in strength and with gusts
it blew first one then another causing them to scurry.
The sun beamed down in delight as the sky cleared
turning to azure tinged with sapphire blue hues.
Yellow warming beaming rays heating the earth
all around are buds springing into life and unfurling.
One by one the petals open and stretch upwards
across the valley a blaze of colour waves in the breeze.
Forgotten now the icy winds and snow of cruel winter
as all about the signs of new life slowly emerges.
Hearts sing along with the playful breeze whisking by
as lambs bleat and skip as they chase each other.
Then tired fall asleep at their mothers feet awhile,
as Spring does her work preparing earth for summer.

Shadow Hamilton

They Call

Moans echo across the lands
from the souls who are lost
drifting, searching, seeking
forever doomed to exile.
Some brought down in their prime
foully murdered by sharpened steel
plunged into them with hatred.
Or maybe by plain greed.
Soldiers killed in needless wars
all for the rape of the innocent.
Governments hungry for more
oil, gold and other things.
Yes too, the souls of creatures
many now extinct voice their
sorrow with despairing moans.
That echo into our minds and hearts.
Mingling together they strike fear
that judders in our very being.
As we huddle in our beds shivering
knowing it is us who caused this damage

Yet Again

Why are you back again?
you keep plaguing me,
creeping up on me
attacking me from within.
Insidiously you invade,
loving my warmth
and my sweetness settling
in, making yourself at home
You attack me slyly
not welcome in the least,
yet you do not care
what damage you do.
Four times now this year
you have invaded me
rushing into my body
germ that you are.
Enough I say, be gone!
find yourself another host.
Leave me alone to recover,
go find yourself someone else.

Shadow Hamilton

Awash With Colour

As I walk around my garden, I note
that my daphnia is in full flower
it is always my first bush to show
and fill my garden with tantalising scent.
My Yucca always gives me colour
in the bleak month of December
standing there so stately
each year another head appears.
The trellis will soon be awash
with its orange trumpets
that brighten up an otherwise dull wall
and makes me smile as they reach up high.
While my various rose bushes
gleefully soon will cover my pergola
mingling with the honeysuckle
filling garden with most delightful scent.
Ah everywhere the promise of Spring abounds
How I long for the warm days to come
when I can sit out by my ponds
and watch fish darting hither and tither.
Dragonflies some enormous and so pretty
visit my lilies and briefly settle there
Spring the month of my birth
will at last soon be here.

Hush

Hush now, listen; do you hear it?
listen carefully, it is all around you,
within the rustle of the leaves
and deep down in the earth.
Tell me what it is you hear?
do you understand this sound?
It is the heart beat of life itself, so
place your hand upon the ground.
Feel the surging beat quietly rumbling
even up in the sky it still beats on
hug the old oak tree, feel the life
within its bark as the sap flows.
Watch the birds and insects
as they flitter by, they too know
and rejoice as they soak up the sun beams.
So pause and listen and you will know too.

written 26 Feb 2015

Shadow Hamilton

Rain Soaked Land

Rain cascading down flooding land
water levels creeping up high
banks blocked with bags of sand
Creeping water flooding moorland
wiping out the fields of rye
rain cascading down flooding land
Homes by pumps are being manned
while folks stand helpless and sigh
banks blocked with bags of sand
While rivers by bridges spanned
lay broken by torrents from sky
rain cascading down flooding land
Man's best laid plans no longer stand
swept away, will it never dry?
banks blocked with bags of sand
And black clouds choked with rain vie
with birds sheltering in the pig sty
rain cascading down flooding land
banks blocked with bags of sand.

Equinox

As the weather softly turns
Beckoning in the Equinox
Clusters of colourful bulbs
Dance and sway in the breeze
Eagles swoop up on thermals
Flying high until they are specks
Golden feathers gleaming amid
Heather glowing white on the hills
Indigo skies with puffy clouds
Jutting into various shapes
Kale drift by lazily snapping flies
Luscious grasses adorn the meadows
Mushrooms appear nestled under trees
Nightingales sweetly sing in Spring
Osprey dive deep for fish
Plunging in time and again
Quaint old-fashioned flowers
Radiant with rainbow colours
Spread rampant in the beds
Tulips dip and bow in greeting
Under the hosta's a dormouse lives
Velvet nose twitching the air
Watching out for birds of prey
Xanado bathed in sunshine highlights
Yellow buttercups which coat the ground as
Zenith of Spring soon now will fade away.

Shadow Hamilton

Magnet

There is a gigantic magnet
somewhere far out in deepest space
that holds the planets in their place
sun and moon too, do rise and set.
All controlled by this magnet
that makes the moon govern the tides
whilst stars do whisper in asides
of this and that caught in its jet.
Yet who controls it, this magnet?
for that one must read the book
and not just skimp but really look
read every word and heaven get.
Our life of free will is governed
by vast things beyond our knowledge
all courses pre-set by a hedge
that path of God to us is wed.

Oops I Slipped Up

Back in the day living a riotous life in London
I used to walk along Park Lane almost nightly
I was living in Paddington but went out in Mayfair
Often as I passed the Grosvenor Hotel there was a ball.
One Night appropriately dressed I gate crashed
Very soon I was asked to dance a waltz
and as we dipped and bowed around the floor
I found out that he was a policeman.
Quickly saying ty I moved on to my next partner
Only to discover that yes he too was a policeman
this set a trend I had only gate crashed the police ball
tail tucked between my legs I beat a hasty retreat.
I suppose the lesson I learned was very important
always be honest in all of your dealings.
It had a large impact on my life over the course of time
taught me values that are now second nature.

Shadow Hamilton

A Tribal War

A tribal War
In a small clearing it stood
dark and majestic against the sky
small silver like veins run riot
across its pitted scarred surface.
Glinting in the sun it sparkled
seeming near alive at times.
Two tribes considered it a god
and warred for the sole rights
to hold their ceremonies at its base.
indifferent to man kinds folly
it stood sentinel to only time,
all this it had seen before.
Two from opposing sides fell in love
and war once more flared up
their love being considered taboo.
No happy ending to this tale
alas they fought 'til all lay dead
And still the meteor rock stood tall.

Nature Visions

The Ostrich

A bird of grandiose stature, he struts the veld
do not anger him for his powerful kick
can main or even kill. Gently he watches
over his brood their mother left long ago.
It falls onto him to incubate their eggs.

Impressive wingspan as he shades his chicks
from the relentless midday scorching sun.
Watch those long legs hammering away
as he chases off a rival who strays too close.
Yet for all his strength and size a pea of a brain
famous for hiding his head in the sand
as if it will make him invisible from sight,
he does look so weird bum stuck up in the air.
Attracted by anything that glitters
he gobbles up all sorts of weird things.
Once tamed his joy is to run in races but rarely
in a straight line as he veers here and there,
oft times leaving mayhem in his wake.
As dusk falls, he gathers up his brood
and struts off into the setting sun
his life is really quite a simple one
with freedom to roam the sunlit veld.

Shadow Hamilton

Winter's End

Slowly, so infinitely slowly
Winter releases his frozen grip.
Gradually the earth starts to warm
only to be plunged back by icy storms
that coat the world in white once more.
Yet inevitably Spring begins to win
as she warms the lands causing new growth.
Snowdrops first show their charming faces
with crocuses close behind sprinkling colour.
Ice finally frees the frozen waters of the lake
and tuneful drips of water strike rocks and soil.
The dull greys of winter now fade away leaving
golden sparkle of sunrays that smilingly beam.
Causing birds to sing as they collect twigs
and fleecy sheep's wool to line their nests.
Busily the insects go to work pollinating
and cleaning up. While the trout gleefully leap
to grab a fat fly and with splash dive down.
The lake gleams in a myriad of colours
blues shot through with silver and purple.
And Winter fades to a distant memory,
near forgotten in the warm Spring days.

written 17 Jan 2015

Nightingale

Nondescript brown bird of renown,
nightly you serenade me.
Golden dulcet tones flood the woods
and I am wafted far away,
off into a wondrous dream world
full of mystical creatures.

written 01/13/2015

Shadow Hamilton

Time Warp

I lay in the bath, scented candles gently waft
tantalising and teasing as the hot water brushes
my skin setting it tingling. I stir my legs and
hands creating rippling waves that set me afire.
I see you approaching through the billowy steam
and hold out my arms in welcome. You tease as
slowly you strip naked giving an odd tantalising
wiggle then lean over and kiss me passionately.
You slide into the bath with me water lapping
over the edge. Our limbs tangle as our lips
meet in hot lingering kisses and we slowly
sink under the surface entwined together.
Gasping I come up and stare around baffled
realising I am on my own, that I had slid under.
Slowly, sadly I realise it was only a dream, a
beautiful moment suspended in another time.
The veils had parted allowing us to love briefly
once more until we are, at last reunited by death.

written 1/11/2015

Circles

Circles, circles always circles
time turning round and round
seasons come and seasons go
and the sky flows endlessly on.
From birth to death turning
circles, circles always circles
spiralling in blaze of colour
the pretty flowers live their cycle.
Relentless is mother nature
as all things she controls in
circles, circles always circles
just keep up with the flow.
A life starts while another ends
as the planets daily keep their cycle
and moon and sun bow to each other
circles, circles always circles.

Shadow Hamilton

Spring Dreams

How my heart longs for spring
with its warm light breezes.
To see the wonders of young buds
slowly unfurling bringing colour.
The promise of new birth all around,
baa of newborn lambs as they skip
through the green lush pastures.
Chasing after each other gleefully.
The happy songs of birds gathering
up wool and twigs to refurbish nests
Some already sitting patiently on eggs
their mate bringing fat worms and goodies.
The longer lighter nights hold promise
of the hot summer that is soon to come.
Spring flowers adorn woods, fields and hedges
and gentle splash of pastel colour fills gardens.
Until Spring gently takes over from Winter
I will dream on wrapped up in woolly fleece.

Nature Visions

Moon Rays

It promised to be a bright starry night
as the sun dipped over the horizon.
Poignantly poised the few clouds scatter
as majestically the moon makes her appearance.
So close as she starts her nightly sweep
her rays near bright as day, regally
she dominates the dark sending it to oblivion as
she highlights this and that according to her whim.
Fickly she slips behind some clouds and
plunges the lands into inky darkness.
Laughing with glee she travels to her zenith
hovering there perfectly framed in beauty.
Now past her apex time rushes on as she dips down
her stellar light slowly begins to fade away.
With a final flick she bathes the world in silver
then bows to the dawning sun as she slips away

Shadow Hamilton

From Sky

It starts off high up in the sky
formed amidst clouds all inky
frozen solid in flakes all spiky
This frozen water falling slowly
some of it all wet and trickily
slowly it hardens so thirstily
More spikes come together
growing whiter and larger
shaping into a frosty layer
Star like now it spirals wildly
pausing a moment briefly
as it settles so blithely
Amidst a fluffy blanket
for all a shining trinket
laid in a white casket
And so the story is finished
with a flake so cherished
until oh so slowly it vanished
Always be true to yourself

Nature Visions

Nativity

As the morning dawned to a world of white
and smoked curled up from chimney pots
Indoors people started to stir and rise
the children excited ran to the tree.
Beneath it, presents in colourful paper
and delightful smells waft from kitchen
All dressed up in their best for church
they file into the pews singing a carol.
The vicar tells the Nativity story as
children act it out.
Then home for their Christmas meal
where father say grace and bids all to
remember the birth of the precious child.
Once the meal is done, it is present time.
First Dad hands one to the youngest
and all watch her joy as she opens it.
Each in turn opens theirs to find
that Santa had answered their dreams.
The vicar tells the Nativity story as
children act it out.
At evening prayers, the message given
is to love one another and always to
walk in Jesus's ways holding him dear
to be kind to all and help when you can.
Back at home after supper it is bedtime
and happy children snuggle under covers,
it has been the best Christmas ever.
But they will carry always the memories.
The vicar tells the Nativity story as
children act it out.

Memoirs

Although born in Scotland I have no memories of there as we left when I was two.
My first recollections are of Las Palmas in the Canaries.
I recall the donkey passing daily and being told he bites.
I was given a caterpillar and tended it, oh so carefully.
My mother when it was a cocoon persuaded me to put it outside.
Well you can imagine my intense disappointment to find
that it had hatched and flown without me getting a single glimpse!!
This is the first disappoint in life that I faced. Our house had a flat roof
with a lovely garden on top and in the distance an enormous, tall chimney.
I remember our boxer Susie she was really crazy especially on the beach
and while breaking open sugar cane it slipped and cut me wide open
right between the right thumb and first finger. I was taken to the doctor
who would you believe? poured iodine into it, he wanted to stitch it too,
but no way
was I letting that sadist anywhere near me again. I still bear the scar today.
I recall seeing a woman dressed in black perched atop of a towering cliff
when we were out in the car my sister saw her too. We had to turn back due to
landslides and she was gone, she also had a pointy hat did we see a witch?
I had a wonderful dolls house into which I could walk, yet I took all my dolls
apart to see how they worked I was such an inquisitive child.
At five we returned to England living very near Hampstead Heath and Parliament
Hill fields. One day when my mother walked me to school I entered to find not
a single soul present so I walked up to my aunts as she lived very close.
Needless to say, I got into a real heap of trouble from both school and mum.
I recollect an outing to Hampstead Heath there was a cafe surrounded by a
large hedge from which I could never find the way out. I ran ahead and
entered through the hedge only to find my parents nowhere to be seen.
Of course, I could not find the way out back to the car. This couple found

me and insisted on taking me to the police station four miles away I kept trying to tell them I only lived two streets down from the Heath, Grown-ups!!!

I remember always wanting to speak Spanish and people refusing to answer me

telling me I had to speak in English Bah! I used to ride my tricycle up and down five stairs mum always telling me I would fall. Well one day my sister called me and I tumbled down breaking my right wrist I used to stuff vegetables

up inside the plaster to avoid eating them. I hate most vegetables to this very day.

When I was seven we got Kim our German shepherd who we took to Africa with us.

I recollect the excitement of visiting Gibraltar and seeing the monkeys, the mystery of sailing through the Suez Canal the banks so close as to seem touchable. A giant ray getting caught on the ships bows oh boy did it stink. It stayed with us from the equator to Zanzibar yuck! I looked on all goggle eyes at the first dark people I had ever seen cowering by my mum as they banished

machetes in the air some with only one eye. I was trembling in my shoes. Kim took a dislike to them as they teased her by poking her with sticks through

her cage. This dislike stayed with her for life. We arrived in Dar-es-Salaam on my eight birthday. From here another tale begins, later to be told.

Shadow Hamilton

Winter Solstice

Winter lashes out with awful fury knowing
the solstice means her time soon will end.
That tail between legs hangs as days lengthen
and land frozen and icy will begin to warm.
Winter's raging blizzards coat land white
with massive drifts of snow that block
passage through the lanes and tracks.
Pristine glittering icicles adorn trees.
Lakes frozen solid, dimly glimpsed fish swim
beneath. While on banks shy snowdrops peek
and carefully open their petals one by one.
Yet still Winter tightens her grip stubbornly.
The days slowly lengthen, and sun warms earth
only to be plunged back into an icy freeze.
For a while longer Winter rejoicing reigns
But Spring will soon relentlessly march in.

Nature Visions

Nice Things

Chocolate ice cream slowly melting
with taste most divine,
sirloin steak well matured frying
tonight well we will dine.
sweet songs from birds singing
greeting the morning sun.
bay mare with mane flowing
chases after the dun.
Mighty trees with branches swaying
give sheltering shade,
tender plants with buds opening
show glimpses of jade.
Puffy white clouds quickly scurrying
across sapphire sky,
sunshine downward is blazing
outlining shadows so inky.
Enjoying a kiss when sunbathing
held close in your arms,
to the top of Dunkery climbing
Wales through mist slowly forms

Shadow Hamilton

A Hush

There was a hush over the land
not even a blade of grass stirred.
The sun beamed down in delight
and flowers opened their petals.
The lake sparkled and shone
its waves lapping the shore.
The odd fish leapt up at flies
then swiftly sunk back down.
The forest trees seemed to part
leaving a faint winding path.
Then into the shady clearing
she daintily stepped out.
As she appeared a ripple,
a ripple of excitement.
Gleaming coat of silver
as the sun highted her.
She stood there poised
as her ears flicked listening.
A sculpture of beauty
with rippling muscles.
It was that most elusive creature
with a spiral horn in her head.
That gracefully walked to drink
when done she faded into shadow
Once more the forest came alive
on the ground a silver hair
giving proof to the legend
that indeed Unicorns still live.

The Old Year

The old year is now done and dusted
It has not been without its strifes.
Headlines of war, murder and much more
Daily we hear of terrible atrosities.
Peace seems a long way off
and Mankind not in the mood.
Yet a spark of hope remains
That one day things will change.
This spark if it is fanned,
could catch alight and burn,
bringing world peace
repairing the harm once done.
People now armed with shovels
replanting all the lost trees.
Animals no longer fearful
turn their trusting eyes to us.
Communities working together
Love for one another freely flowing.
Slavery a thing of long distant past
All this could come to pass.
We just need enough to care
To want to make a change.
Then like the mighty oak,
the seeds will take deep roots.
Just one person who cares
can influence many others
And this world of ours
will once more be paradise.

Written 13 Dec 2014

Shadow Hamilton

Festivity

I have seen Millennia in
and now its twenty fifty
I somehow made my century
rejoicing with my family.
It has passed it seems
in the mere eye blink.
Now I reminisce
held close in loving arms
Festivity floods the senses
stores groaning with toys.
Butchers laden with meat
people scurrying hither and thither.
Shop fronts all lit up
with flashing decorations.
Children's eyes on beanstalks
wish lists growing bigger.
Fridges crammed to the brim
with tempting tasty treats.
Good will for neighbours
as carol singers' carousal.
Mothers sweating over stoves
as Dad mixes up eggnog.
Presents colourfully wrapped
adorn Christmas trees feet.
At end of day, happy faces
and a few groaning bellys,
people falling into bed
T'is all done for another year

written 12 Dec 2010

Nature Visions

I Dream

I dream of fluffy white clouds
sailing across vibrant skies,
of hidden worlds trapped within
gently, softly blanketed.
I dream I am in a bubble
floating up higher and higher,
until at last I mingle in clouds
and step out into ravishing beauty.
I dream of floating castles
with silver and gold turrets,
a moat with golden swans
that carry me to the castle.
I dream of a tall handsome man
standing there with hand extended,
my own prince charming, who
sweeps me up and carries me inside

Shadow Hamilton

Spare a Thought

Spare a thought this time of year
for them who have no-one to care
no roof overhead and no fare
life on streets hard to bear
Spare a thought to those alone
tucked up indoors no-one calls
between societies cracks falls
and lay there abandoned stone
Spare a though for those at war
fighting for friends and family
no roses for them just a lily
lays on a grave like a mar
Spare a thought, yes spare a thought

Nature Visions

Jack Frost

Jack Frost laid his hand over the lands
trees now adorned with hoar frost gems
laughing in glee watched people slip
then slide helpless down the slopes.
Bitter cold from his fingers ran
turning the ground rock hard
as icicles grew so very long
the air so brittle it snapped.
Surveyed his domain unsatisfied
and pointed a slender finger
windows now became jammed
locks too now frozen solid.
Yet as the sun rose up high
Jack Frost's work became undone
and back into oblivion he slipped
knowing there was always next year.

Shadow Hamilton

Santa

Santa so fat in chimney got stuck
swearing and hot he got in a muck
kicking up much soot
boot fell off his foot
that night he was sure right out of luck

written 30 Nov 2010

Victims

This world of ours is not always a good place
behind closed doors so many terrible things occur.
Hidden from plain sight some suffer endless torture
by the very ones who should love them the most.
Terrible things done sometimes in loves name
horrific beatings handed out, just for the sake of control.
Murders committed simply because one person will not share
killing so no-one else can take their supposed loved one away.
Children living in fear beaten and starved flinching at loud voices
creeping round like little mice hoping praying they are not noticed.
Gangs that bully and terrorise neighbourhoods while selling drugs
slashing up rival gangs purely for more territory to increase their strangle hold
to continue their evil crimes. Young girls and boys sold into sexual slavery,
victims each and every one and all for profit. War torn countries
full of horrendous abuse, dead and injured cast aside like trash.
Yet for each who deals out these horrible crimes once they were
different, once they were loved. Can all be explained away by the fact
that they were taught by those that reared them in these horrific circumstances?
Or is it true that some were born monsters who enjoy other's pain and grief?
Practicing their craft on helpless victims as they grow up pulling wings of birds
slicing and dicing up beloved pets. Always attacking the weak and helpless.
Plain bullies that carry out their crimes in secret afraid to face those of strength.
One never really knows what goes on behind those closed doors.
Yet when a victim finally snaps and turns the tables oft times they are the ones our systems
punish and lock away behind bars while their tormentor is left free to continue
their rampage. Who I ask is the beast? Mankind surely deserves this name not animals.

Shadow Hamilton

Átstan Impresario

An Angelo Arab, you had immense spirit
dappled grey with a huge leap over fences.
Your stable name was Tom, pedigree name
too much of a mouthful for every day use.
In your stable you were a terror to my grooms
pulling faces and hunching up your back as if
to bite or even kick. It was all show you just
wanted to be left alone, a true one-person horse.
No other could ride you as you would buck and buck
even going down and rolling to get rid of other riders.
Shoes could be a challenge as you would snatch feet away
or refuse to lift them up, only one blacksmith did you tolerate.
Yet to me and my mother you were so sweet, nickering
a welcome when you saw either of us coming.
You floated over fences winning us many rosettes
when turned out you would race down the jumping lane.
With Sheroake at your heels laughing with glee
you would go up and down time and again.
Then take delight in having a long dusty roll
finally settling down to graze the sweet grass.
Fast as a flash, the clock never a challenge
perfect rounds nearly every single time.
In one year you went from grade C to grade A
barely 14:3 hands tall yet heart of a giant.

You always held a special place in my heart
many the hours we spent together out riding
or practicing in the paddock, at dressage
you were a real ace act graceful as a swan.
Tom sweet Tom how I loved you
maybe the more as only I alone
on your back you would tolerate
your love made me feel so proud

Nature Visions

Great spirit horse long may you race
the clouds where you now dwell
If I close my eyes I can still hear
the thundering of hooves flying by.
Never again was there a horse
quite like you. I remember your neat
little ears flickering back and forth
as I spoke to you, with a nicker you
would answer me and toss your head.

Shadow Hamilton

No Shame Or Blame

There is no blame or shame
in sometimes not being the same.
Woes will oft times call our name
even if we live a life without blame.
The secret is to play the game
whilst our hearts we tame
giving the finger to the dame
of misfortune who is in the frame.
Revoking things of ill fame
bad things we set aflame
and their sins we disclaim.
It is all about playing the game.
So come forward without shame
you are who you are, so your life reclaim
and at the end of the day proclaim
to all, I am me without any blame.

Nature Visions

Winds of the World

Pampero you rush across the pampas of Argentina
blowing fast and strong bending all before you.
Mighty and powerful you make your presence known
as you travel o'er the pampas in triumphant passage.
Ah Simoom you shift around the sand dunes
sucking up all moisture as you journey the Sahara,
creating vast clouds of blinding sand. Stinging
sands that cut like knives tearing at clothes.
Tramontane you blow so cold as you traverse
the Alps bringing with you freezing ice and snow.
And flick over to the Pyrenees where you dance
in delight as you blow hard and strong whipping up snow.
Wreck house you blow down the slopes of the Range mountains
of Newfoundland. Cleansing and refreshing as you bring
life giving rains to their slopes. Vibrant greens left by your path
as you go on to who knows quite where
Fremantle Doctor you are an afternoon sea breeze
coming in from the Indian Ocean you bring
welcome coolness across Perth with a salty tang,
but only in the summer months do you work your charms.
Plough winds breezing along in straight furrows
preceding thunderstorms forming clusters of rain.
No deviation in your path straight as a arrow
you bring lightning flashes that lit the skies.
Calima the dread of housewives as you bring
dust laden clouds to the shores of the Canary Islands,
coming south to southeasterly carried by the
Saharan air layer. The sooner gone the better.
Abrolhos with your frequent squalls that traverse
in the months of May through to August known in
Portuguese as open eyes you flow between
Cabo de San Tome and Cabo Frio causing chaos.

written 2014

Darkness

Darkness stalked through the shadowed lands
only briefly glimpsed before vanishing.
It passed through valleys and ridges leaving
in its wake despair and torment and Blood soaked lands.
No friend of light, it kept to the dark paths
releasing disharmony and malcontent in its wake.
No respecter of life's beauty, its intent most malice
feeding on people's fears and greed, it gained in strength.
A veritable feast lay before it as it advanced
and used man's foibles to its personal gain.
Causing strife and friction was its delight
setting one against another chuckling with glee.
Yet, where there is darkness there is also light
and it is daily pushed back into the shadowed lands
from whence it came. Once again it is conquered
by both light and the spring of eternal hope.

Autumn Oak Tree

Majestically stretching high
nude of leaf, its structure plainly seen

written 22 Nov 2014

Shadow Hamilton

Friendship

To make friends with someone is
to start a new adventure.
You can find good friends in unlikely places
and when you least expect to.
Friendship is the art of caring
and also of giving freely in return.
There is a sense of wellbeing as
you awake and remember you meet today.
A chance to catch up and share gossip
to connect again with each other.
A good friend is one of the biggest treasures
that one can have and needs nurturing.
I value highly my friends to the extent
that I will drop everything to help them.
Or just to be there as their shoulder
when they need someone to lean on.
Friendship is especially about bad times
knowing your friend will come through for you.
Never underestimate the power of friendship
everything else is just daily details.

Loneliness

Loneliness was losing you ten years ago
I now wake up each day your side empty
I miss the cuddles and early morning sex
the endless hours without your smile.
No-one to share special moments with.
At night once the door shuts others out and
the long hours creep by each one darker
It is now I again feel the isolation.
No-one to share a joke or smile with,
in others minds you are now forgotten
yet for me it is still like yesterday.
Endless hours stretching out, on and on.
No-one to hold me when I weep in despair
or to wipe away the tears and comfort me.
I smile when people visit, offer some tea
but deep inside the tears never stop.
People tell me it's time to forget,
well, that would mean cutting out my heart.
For without you I am less than nothing
It is all the memories that comfort me.
The joyous times we together shared
and the life we lived together harmoniously.
My heart still belongs to you, none measure up
how could they? You and you alone are my soul.
So resigned I live with loneliness
fill my days with things to do.
Taking comfort in friends and family
Yet once the door closes loneliness sets in.

Written 19 Nov 2014

Shadow Hamilton

A Mote of Dust

A mote of dust travels through the air
blown this way and that across the lands.
Finally after many miles it is entrapped
in a rocky crevasse where it joins others.
In time the wind blows in many more motes
and something wondrous starts happening.
These motes give birth to little plants
that struggle at first then bind the land.
Encouraging new birth all around and
flowers that vibrantly wave in the breeze.
Young saplings shoot out deep tap roots
that anchor them in place where they flourish.
In time a mighty forest springs to life
harbouring a wealth of flora and fauna.
All of this came to pass due to just one,
one solitary mote of well-travelled dust.

written 18 Nov 2014

Nature Visions

Him

With his cup full to the brim
he sat there looking grim
He had come here on a whim
his intention to have a swim.
Yet now he had lost his vim
perhaps he left it at the gym.
About his figure he liked it trim
and his hair he kept very prim.
His knees he would skim
as trees he tried to shim.
As daylight started to dim
he went home via the rim.

Shadow Hamilton

Winter Days

Gone, now just a memory the warmth of summer,
winter's icy fingers now take a harsh grip turning
land to frozen waste. Blanketing it in snow as the
nights draw in, reflecting the bright moon.
Children having fun sledges rushing down the hill
and snowmen appear standing as sentinels to winter.
The whisk of skiers as they fly past speeding downwards
their colourful ski suits adding splashes of vivid colour.
Jack Frost hard at work decorating trees with icicles
some short and others long sparkling, reflecting light
appearing like gems amidst the sprinkled snow covered
branches. Once more winter reigns supreme.
Icy winds howl across the valleys causing drifts
of snow some eight foot deep, chilling bones
making us huddle down in fleece lined coats
Rosy cheeks blaze out from under hoods,
And fingers freezing cold from handling snow.
contentment in every face as people head home.
To cups of hot chocolate and toasty warm fires
shutting out for now winter's icy blast.

Nature Visions

Dank Pants

A fisherman sat with line all lank
perched on crooked stool that soon sank
backside now all mud covered
his face an embarrassed red
off home he went with his pants all dank.

13 Nov 2014

Shadow Hamilton

A Turning Point

The man stumbled on, wanting to get as far away as possible
the sights he had seen and lived through too terrible to contemplate.
How could another human deliberately inflict such awful things on another.
He could see a gentle stream of smoke arising from the distant chimney
and headed for the shelter it offered, staggering on until he reached it.
It was a pretty cottage nestled deep into the hillside and isolated.
He tumbled through the door and collapsed on the floor.
Mistily he drifted in then out of consciousness unable to focus
aware vaguely of a gentle touch that soothed and replenished.
He drank from the cup pressed to his lips and then let go.
The old lady shook her head at the follies of mankind,
and set to work bandaging his festering wounds.
She made a drawing potion to clean out the poison
that had taken a fierce hold racking him with fever.
Then she covered him and stoked up the fire.
For three days he lay in a coma muttering about the war,
not an ordinary one, oh no, this war caused carnage.
Evil stalked the land every hand turned against the other.
Sons killing fathers and brothers and to what point?
A simple disagreement about Creed had started this.
Weakened by the ravages he was slow to fully heal
yet he learned much from the old lady causing him to rethink.
To look at things with eyes a-new seeing the other point of view.
These new values he took with him when he left thanking her gratefully.
He set out on a new route, his task now to heal and bring peace.
Standing a-midst the crowd on a small hillock he taught them new values
not by preaching as such but by parables that showed the way to peace.
After all he would say; Pause and Think, For What are We without hope?
Everything gone by can be changed, all we have to do is care and act.
So lit the small flicker in your heart and fan up a healing blazing flame.

Chopped 11

I sit by the open window watching out for hubby's return.
The ancient oil lantern sways casting pools of light.
There are insects buzzing around it, they seem to be playing kamikaze.
Some pay the price as they get zapped, others seemingly to live charmed life.
As I sit waiting enjoying the night sounds, a large moth appears by the window
so close I could touch it. Then it starts its crazy yet enchanting dance.
Flitting first up and down, now going round and round.
Mottled browns and reds adorn wings of glossier like silks.
Alone like me it seems to be yet having fun drawing weird patterns.
It gets closer to the glass on each pass, a dancing dare devil of beauty.
I do not want to see it zapped, so go out and turn of the lantern.
Sitting in the old rocker chair, I gaze into the star-studded sky.
And there silhouetted is my moth
as it flies away across the moon.
Free to live another day and night
it is joined by another as hubby arrives.

written 8 Nov 2014

Shadow Hamilton

I Am

I am a whisper in the breeze
I am a mote of dust blown by said wind
I am everything yet also nothing
I am a tree stretching for the sky
I am the cloud that momentarily hides the sun
I am the life giving morning dew
I am the shadow flitting past
I am the words that I write
I am the visions others see in them
I am the sweet smelling flowers
I am nothing yet everything
I am, I am just me, warts and all
I am female

Written 06 Nov 2014

Flashing Eyes

Flashing eyes hot with fury
she stalked up to him
furiously they argued
as she pushed and shoved him.
Catching hold of her wrists
he rode out her fury.
As she calmed, he kissed
her with desire and passion.
At first, she weakly pushed
him, struggling to be free.
Then with gentle sigh
she gave into his demands.
Now matching him with rising passion
she voluptuously returned his kisses.
As ardent as she had been furious
together they sank down melded together.
Their tender cries softly whispered
as their volcanic love fiercely burned.
Then drained to the core they snuggled
each content in the other's arms.

Shadow Hamilton

Day Break

The sun slowly rises over the horizon
casting its rays turning night to day.
Chasing away the lingering darkness
revealing the hills and shadow cast valleys.
Details become more apparent showing
the pretty flowers and stately trees.
With lake's waters glistening brightly
reflecting the beaming sun rays.
Peace of day now shattered by
the raucous chorus of crows.
As dipping down they fly
mugging the other birds.
Soon scattering at gunfire
from the farmers crop scarers.
Joyful tunes now abound
As song birds sing out their hearts
Welcoming dawn's warm rays
hustle and bustle as people awake
and tranquillity slips away
as dawn becomes full day.

Nature Visions

Yesterday's Joys

Yesterday's joys come flooding back,
memories that stir the senses
that leave me bereft for their lack.
Yet still their joy punches a whack,
that set a stir in my pulses.
Yesterday's joys come flooding back.
And so I gather up my sack,
full to brim with loving senses
that leave me bereft for their lack.
Joyous feeling my heart do rack
once more loving without lapses.
Yesterday's joys come flooding back.
No longer dressed in dark black,
I, now leave behind all senses
that leave me bereft for their lack.
Stuffed full of joyful glimpses,
my sack holds passionate senses.
Yesterday's joys come flooding back
that leave me bereft for their lack.

written 02 Nov 2014

Shadow Hamilton

Near Death Experience

Back when I was twelve, my dad built me a dabchick
I had great fun learning how to sail it getting many dunking's
Us kids used to sail around the harbour and race to the spit.
One day after racing back and forth several times,
the wind started to pick up and the others headed ashore.
But I carried on, this was way too fun as I sped about.
The squall grew stronger, and I turned turtle several times
up righting my boat I foolishly carried on until as I up ended her
I was hit on the head, dazed I sat on the up turned hull.
Unable in the squall's strength to get her up right
I clung to the centre board and watched the harbour wall get closer
too dazed to realise the danger I was in I just sat there waiting.
Lucky for me the yacht club notified the life boat and it came out,
rescued in the nick of time they took me aboard and dried me off.
They towed my dabchick still turned turtle back to the yacht club.
My parents Dad especially were furious and I was grounded for
the rest of the summer while dad repaired my dabchick.
My humiliation was complete when the local paper covered my rescue.
I learnt that day to respect the sea and treat it with caution.
My story could have ended so differently. Yet I remained a dare devil
and went through two very bad car clashes with barely a scratch.
Now at last much wiser I take things much more steadily
and rarely take such risks after all I am not invincible.
Just someone who pushed her luck right to the edge.

written 2 Nov 2014

Take Over

For weeks now the two young males had been watching,
waiting for their opportunity and now it was time.
They were now strong enough to take over the pride.
Signalling his intent to his brother Moto stood up
and started forward with Javier following behind.
As the reached the pride a battle royal ensued
The lionesses desperate to drive them off knowing
if they succeeded vast changes would occur.
Far in the distance Soto heard the roars and growls
as the take over ensued and rushed to protect them.
The fight was long and hard with some fatalities.
Soto received wounds that would take months to heal
as he was banished by the brothers, his life now as an outcast.
Luckily for him Zanidar joined him with her cubs of nearly a year old
She and they would keep him fed as he slowly healed.
Back at the pride the brothers set about their gruesome task
all the cubs were hunted down and killed without mercy.
Now the lionesses would soon be ready to mate again
and it would be their blood that the offspring would bear
perpetuating their line and increasing the size of the pride.
Life in the African Savannah was always cruel and hard
the brothers would face many challengers in their time.
Food always an issue once the migrating herds moved on.
Now a time of little the pride suffered and grew weaker.
The only saving grace was the buffalo not without their risks.
Valiant fighters who protected each other forming a ringed barrier
around the more vulnerable, ready to fight to the death.
With very young cubs the lionesses needed food to feed them
and desperation drove them on, finally they made a good kill
none would go hungry for a few days. In the distance the clouds
gathered rain falling far up country at last reaching them and
with the rain the vast herds once more returned and life teemed.
Now was a time of plenty and the pride recovered their health.

Shadow Hamilton

For seven years the brothers ruled supreme yet in the background there were many waiting their own time. Two males in particular Janto and Batso sons of Soto watched and waited eager to take over until at last it was their time and turn to roust the pride males. And so the never ending cycle started again until the next time.

Savannah Night

There was an uneasy feeling that night on the savannah.
The creatures were jumpy as they huddled and grazed.
Startling at each new sound, one stamps its foot and
the vast herd flees, from what they are unsure.
The lions creep through the long grass setting an ambush.
The first pair's job to spook the herd now is done.
The rest spread out, now taking up the deadly hunt.
Working quickly, they target one and separate it.
One lioness jumps on its back then slips off and is trampled.
Another tackling it face on is gored in the shoulder.
But the rest soon have it cornered and it is soon smothered.
As it dies the pride are already ripping open its belly.
The blood covers the land red as it seeps into the soil
There will be feasting tonight as the lions gather to eat.
Snarling as they rip into the warm carcass, blows lashing out,
As they vie for position, pushing and shoving each other.
The hunt was long and hard, the fruits came at high price.
Two lionesses wounded, one will die. Such is the cost of success.
A calf bawls for its mother, yet she cannot answer its call.
Sadly, it is too young to live, it will end up a tasty morsel.
Sated the lions rest in the early sunlight as cubs play.
Life for now on the savannah continues, and peace reigns.

Shadow Hamilton

Day To Night and Back

I watch the sun grow dim,
as it passes through the sky.
Glowing rays start to fade away.
Dipping its beams over the ocean.
Sinking down into its watery depths.
The day now turns to dusk.
Slowly the moon peeks out,
casting earth with silvery light.
Stars blaze in full glory.
Now the nocturnal beings appearing.
Rustling noises emerge from undergrowth.
Owls can be heard,
their hoots ringing out.
A whoosh of wings,
as they sweep by.
Innoxiously night passes.
Dawn creeps in.
Chasing shadows away.
Sun rises,
dawn becomes
Day.

Written 14 Oct 2014

Faith Healer

The old faith healer carefully got things ready.
She had spring water collected from the source
that had been taken at the night of the new moon.
Some special herbs also gathered by moonlight.
Setting the pebbles in a circle on the cleared earth.
She lights a small fire in its heart and feeds it.
Once it is burning bright, she shakes out some of the herbs
adding them to the spring water, then patiently waits.
When the moon appears she busily goes to work,
a pinch of liverwort, some ground sunflowers.
Tansy and dried apple, a bit of spiders web,
she places the pot on the fire and stirs.
First three stirs clockwise, now two anti three more clockwise.
Chanting softly as she stirs the simmering brew.
Now adding crushed primrose and burdock, she stirs.
Then she lays it in the moonlight waiting for dark.
Once the moon slides from sight, she pours it into a vessel
and caps it tight. Shrugging back her hood she gathers all.
Now it is time for it to sit and infuse before it is time for use.
Her fame is renown, the kingdom wide, many are they who seek her.
She blesses the potion first with Mut, then calls on Pax,
finally, she invokes Serena's help, finally done,
she sets it in a ray of moonlight leaving it for now.
It is time for the cleansing of her patients before they drink it.
The following day miraculous recoveries by them all.
Singing her praises they try to cross her hand with silver.
Gently she shakes her head, not for money is her gift.
Freely she shares it, for the goddesses gave her the healing gift.
Mut is the goddess of nature mother earth.
Pax is the goddess of peace.
Serena is the goddess of healing.

written 14 Oct 2014

Shadow Hamilton

Chill Night

'T was a bitter chill night, the stars flooded the clear skies,
then hoar frost formed dressing up the trees with sparkling icicles.
The fragrant apple tree wood merrily burned in the hearth,
sending dancing shadows up and down the walls as if giving birth.
't is Halloween Nite and porches full of flickering pumpkin light.
The children dressed in costumes masks that tinkle bright.
Trick or treat they chant at each door passing tests with a plume.
Returning with many treasures and rewards to their home.
Hark the clock strikes midnight; now is time for ghosts and ghouls,
for the unwary to learn fast, stay indoors or you will lose your soul.

My Owner

I trot after her and settle on my bed in the kitchen.
Knowing first she will feed the humans, then the cats.
I will only be yelled at if I get underfoot, finally
Getting my breakfast I slowly scoff it down.
Owner is yelling at me, what did I do? Oh I am in the way!
Shuffling around deciding which bed I prefer today.
Driving owner mad as I circle and circle then flop down.
After all I must make sure I have scared off all snakes.
Time to go out I bound along at owners side
wanting to get there first being checked back to heel.
Can owner not understand I should go first to protect
the household from any dangers lurking?
Yelling command on top of command, so confusing I close my ears.
One word at a time please if you want me to listen!
Remember Human language is not my own tongue I need time
to assimilate translate and then to finally obey.
Does owner not understand the more frantic they become
the higher state of alert this pushes on me I can not relax.
If owner is so tense and concerned there must be peril lurking.
At last home owner slowly relaxes and I come down from high alert.
This Mexican man stopped by and with him I did click,
He spoke my language and understood where I was coming from.
He taught my owner and showed how to dealt with things calmly.
Oh boy yes Life is much better due to Caesar Milan.

Shadow Hamilton

Cowboys In the Badlands

Rather lost, they stare over the divide,
how best to circumnavigate this obstacle?
They can see a path gently sloping down
but it is far off to the north two days ride.
West is back from whence they had come,
east is an impassable cliff of sheer rocks.
They cannot see far to the south but maybe,
they talk it over and head into the unknown.
Tumble weed rolling by pushed by the wind
as playfully it blows them into their path.
Miniscule trees dot the flat plateau
and small shrubs popping up here and there.
In a hurry they head on swiftly southwards
and soon start to descend to the valley below.
Billy is pale with anxiety as they push on
his wife Betty is due to give birth.
Sammy casts worried looks at his friend knowing
there is little he can say that will help.
At last, they reach the valley and gallop on
Just another five miles will they make it in time?
Their horses now struggling, sweat pouring off them.
Billy's homestead comes into view cattle scattering
as they gallop through the herd and into the yard.
Sammy hangs back as Billy dashes in to Betty.
In full labour she screams "Where have you been?"
"The preacher is here to wed us. Did you get the ring?"
"I have it here" said Billy and without delay they were married.
And within minutes the twins arrived a boy and girl both bawling.
"Geezers you cut that close Billy" said Sammy
as they slumped on the front porch drinking beer.
"We made it in the nick of time" replied Billy
flushed with the joy and fulfilment of life.

written 17 Sept 2014

Nature Visions

In the Desert

Endlessly the golden red tinged sands roll on,
vast dunes tower with narrow gully's betwixt them.
Cast in purple and black shadows harbouring an oasis.
Dotted with swaying palms and colourful birds singing
and blue waters that entice as they shimmer and sparkle.
Here, hidden in the dune's folds, a priceless peace reigns.
A place that holds a treasure not governed by gems or gold.
Here tucked away everyday values no longer are important.
Tranquillity blows in on hot winds that ripple the surfaces
of sand whipping it into mini swirls that dance away.

written 16 Sept 2014

Shadow Hamilton

Death Calls

I see you there, for me waiting,
you hover in endless patience,
now I pass, death me is calling.
Yet I linger on, each breath rasping,
as I am clearing my conscience,
I see you there, for me waiting.
Too soon the curtains are parting,
now at an end is my patience,
now I pass, death me is calling.
Time is slowing, it's so daunting,
draining away is my essence.
I see you there, for me waiting.
Grievances now aside casting,
Letting in instead, some cogence,
now I pass, death me is calling.
Death I have treated with voidance,
giving it little reverence,
I see you there, for me waiting,
now I pass, death me is calling.

Zincograph Plate

As I walk the scented paths through
Beautiful bright flowers that entice.
Capturing memories in their folds I,
Dream of times now past and gone
Each one in itself a treasure to savour.
Fondly I recall such special times,
Heavenly hours spent with you
In blissful moments we shared.
Jealously I hold them to my heart.
Keening softly to myself, my
Love for you will always abound.
Magical fantasy's come in my dreams.
Now never in this life to again share,
Or to be able to hold you near, in
Passions throngs once more.
Quintessential desires burn deep,
Racing through my veins,
Setting me still on fire.
Tortuously teasing, driving me mad,
Understanding, not at all why?
Vacant still my heart remains
With longings unsatisfied.
Xenoglossia people can not us reunite.
Zincograph print is all that now remains.

Shadow Hamilton

Shades of Autumn

The leaves coated the ground in a tapestry of colour,
strewn around like matting hiding all sorts beneath.
A woven carpet that blanketed the earth with hues
of Autumn colours as slowly they returned to dust.
The trees seeming ten times taller without their cladding,
reaching, stretching high branches stark and bare
Knots now clearly seen as they twist this way and that
forming complex shapes high up in the grey skies.
The ground now cooling with Summer long forgotten.
A light sprinkling of frost slowing melting in weak sunlight.
Forming icicles that adorn like sparkling jewellery all a-glitter.
And the cold North wind sweeps over the hills and Vales.
Now all turn dormant, curled up in their winter dens and drays.
Hibernating the cold stark months away, food stashed close to hand.
The temperature falls day by day and in sweeps the snow not settling yet.
As the hours pass it slowly blankets the ground in pristine white.
Winter has now arrived and claimed all as her own!

Nature Visions

The End Is Nigh

As days get shorter and night stretches out.
Summer fades away and earth gets colder.
Soon, Oh too soon snow will again rule and
the earth will slumber under its folds.
Until then we enjoy the fruits of bounty
smelling the last of sweet summer flowers.
Crops stand ready in the fields for collection
Combined harvesters busily at work.
Fat stalks of golden corn, rye and barley
tied in bundles ready for threshing.
Seductive scents of apples waft
as down they are laid for storing.
Frosts now lay the land bare
as the leaves part company
some red, some yellow, others orange
they blow and scatter in the wind.
Trees looking stark and bleak gaze
o'er the stripped fields with snow sprinkling
the now barren ground and soon Winter
will once more rule in her glory
Gone now the lazy days of Summer
her flowers and perfumes distant memories.
Now the hues of colour are subdued.
And all around the land sleeps on.

Shadow Hamilton

A Thing Called Love

This thing that they call love cannot be measured
it comes to us all whether we want it or not.
Sneaking up it hits us in the eyeballs and
turns our lives around giving us both strength
and at the same it makes our knees bend in weakness.
This thing called love has the power to move obstacles
to ease our way. It makes people see life afresh.
It is a feeling that brings wellbeing into daily life.
We are now responsible for another person and our path
together can be sometimes rocky we learn to take
the rough with the smooth trying always to better ourselves.
It makes the world go around as it pushes us ever on
A feeling that tingles our spine as the loved one draws near.
When we love it opens new doors and gives a sense of sharing
and we become more tolerant of the foibles of others faults.
This thing called love gives us so much joy if we let it in.
Remember how it welled up when your first child was born.
Filling our hearts to breaking point as we gaze down and also
filling us with strength and determination to be our best.
To make a good life for our offspring after all it is through
them that eventually we will live on.
Love comes in all shapes and sizes. Never should it be measured,
to measure it is to belittle it and make it small. Accept this gift
with open heart for this is truly what life is about. It is said,
that love conquers all and this I believe, many are life's battles
and loneliness and solitude weaken the human spirit.
Welcome always with open arms this thing called love
let your eyes and heart open, enjoy the small things
nature has to offer. They will enrich your life and enhance
your very soul. Take pride in your achievements, forget
your disaster's, they only matter if you let them and then fester
souring all that should be good and pulling you down.
Yes open wide both heart, eyes and arms and even though
you can not quantify and pin it down just rejoice that we have
this thing called love. Ah Yes it is "la mort" and also "l' amore."

Nature Visions

In Love's Shadow

There is peace in my heart
as I gaze into the fire embers
room full of shadows that sway
as the final flame flickers.
It is now in the quiet of night
as the rest of the world sleeps
that you come to me; again, we love
sharing times past we lay together.
In shadow time the veils fall away.
Once more our world's touch.
Again, we are together in spirit,
now living in the shadow of love.
Yet always the shadows beckon,
enticing me, exciting me, pulling
ever deeper into their depths
and as I slumber, we are reunited.

Shadow Hamilton

Under the Surface

The world daily sees our face,
but only the one we choose.
Under its surface lurk many more.
Emotions a plenty hidden away
beneath the one we show to all,
many are the ripples on its surface.
This mask we show to all smiling,
keeping eighty per cent hidden.
True emotions kept locked up.
What is it we fear? Apathy?
Disgust? Betrayal? or Pain?
Yet under the surface we are safe!
Distrust leads to our hidden face.
A fear of not being accepted
if we show what is under the Surface.
Not always has it been this way.
Life's trials have brought it about.
Yet! Nature herself lives on the surface!

Remnants of Love

Remnants of Love
Nearly ten years since you were called away,
yet still I recall as yesterday your touch,
Your smile, your sense of fun and joy with life.
I remember you playing your guitar, singing along.
You cooking a gourmet meal with great a-plume.
Sharing a bottle of wine over cards or backgammon.
You filled my life with the sunshine of love as
together we shared glances at a humorous joke.
We shared daily strife's with practiced ease
facing each and all together standing strong.
Still I feel your touch in night's shadows
as you softly flit by reminding me of us.
Lonely now is life as I travel onwards,
none can take your place within my heart.
Some good men have tried, yet they can never
be you or be able to share life with your ghost.
Yet as I pause, remembering all you taught me
and experiences we had together I am happy.
Sometimes in life less is indeed far more
now I treasure the memories we made together

written 26 Aug 2014

Shadow Hamilton

A Naked Beauty

She stood there in all her naked beauty,
the man approached her with reverence,
as he stood in front of her drinking in
her exquisite womanhood with awe struck wonder.
Gently he runs his fingers up and down her
searching out her body and crevices.
Pausing here and there lightly stroking
finding her hidden imperfections.
Taking out his hammer and chisel
he gently chips away her blemishes.
Smoothing the marble surface as he goes.
At last satisfied he stands back admiringly.
She glows in the fading sunlight,
seeming to come to life as dusk falls.
the sculptor sighs with pleasure.
It was worth the many hours of work

Nature Visions

Through the Mist

The mist swirls through the trees giving a odd glimpse
of vague shapes that seem to fade and reappear briefly.
Mysterious rustles as gentle breezes form the mist into
oh, so many different things of all shapes and sizes.
Imagination runs riot as mythical creatures seem to
once more walk openly yet camouflaged within the mist.
I reach out and stroke a shy Unicorn on its neck and briefly it
rests its head on my shoulder, then fades back into the mist.

written 20 Aug 2014

Shadow Hamilton

Piano Visions

I sit and listen with awe as the pianist coaxes
the most wondrous sounds from the beat up piano
his melodies flood out greeted by stunned silence
as people are transported into the visions he plays
The music soars filling the room
deepening and expanding
whispering of unseen things
of valley's, mountains and glens
the notes lead us into the glen
revealing the wondrous sights
of waterfall tinkling in time
to the most seductive beat
One can hear the birds singing
their notes blending so harmoniously
with the pianist's various moods
as he swings into blues and jazz
Yet still he plays on notes ringing out
telling oh so many fabulous stories
the silence of the audience says it all
he has transported us to another plane

Nature Visions

Skirl of the Piper

There was an awful caterwauling and clamour
as the pipes filled up with air and swirled
today it was for an orange march
playing the protestant songs of inflammatory verse.
Many were the songs and events the piper was called to skirl
one day it would be dirges the next for highland dances
where amidst the laughter the pipes sang their tunes
some were ballads of times long gone, others were clan songs
Once he had played for a royal wedding in Balmoral castle
now that was a grand occasion with the final dance of swords
pretty girls kicked up their heels showing the odd glimpse
of underwear neath their kilts whilst their sash's flew freely
Nimbly they stepped around the sword circle
high on pointed toes for all like ballerina's
and still the pipes skirled as the piper blew the notes
the bag wheezing with the effort and force of air
Red faced he played on for hours downing the odd dram
to keep his lips a-pucker and to fire his blood
until at last all were done and sat quiet around the fire
and agreeing it had been a grand Ceilidh as the piper rested.
The pipes now quiet and deflated stood in the corner
tomorrow at dawn they would again skirl welcoming the sun
as over the horizon it slowly crept darkness changing to light
until there it was in all its glory greeted royally by the skirling pipes
Ceilidh is a Scottish folk gathering where much whisky is downed and many
reels are danced made more joyous by a good piper skirling and tall stories
told.

Shadow Hamilton

Wanderer

He was a wandering man that travelled many miles
staying a few days here and there, sometimes a week or two
then his feet would get that familiar itch and on he'd go
searching new horizons for his elusive dream.
A lady in every town he visited, sighed, when he travelled on
although he found them all enchanting, with none could he settle
the call of the road was just too strong, and those feet would itch
wondrous sights he found as the roads led him ever onwards.
In the lake district he loved the open spaces and towering hills
the sparkling lakes that nestled like gems at their feet
the air that invigorated his soul with its fresh crispness
to here he often returned and just soaked in the beauty.
In the peaks he found a place from which seven counties were visible
finding out it was for sale, he laid down his money and the deal was done
a simplistic house he built made of cobb and oak that blended into the hills
yet still those feet would itch and off he once more would go.
The years passed by; often he returned for a month or two
he found he was getting slower and inclined to linger in places longer
then one day on the road he caught up to a fellow traveller
that night they lingered around a camp fire sharing stories.
Oh the stories they both had could fill several books with wondrous memories
she had been travelling for 30 years he a bit longer, yet until now
never with another, both had always been solitary by choice
he took her to his home in the dales and shortly after they wed
Still every two to three months they would share a glance
and each would know the others feet felt that age old itch
so forth they would set off to discover new horizons once more
safe in the knowledge they had each other and their cottage awaiting their return

Exquisitely Enchanting

Yet these seconds brought exquisite joy
as I watched my young daughter playing with her toys
so peaceful she looked, yet tense too as she played
her concentration intense, she was in a world of her own.
Then rising she flings herself at me laughing with glee
as she babbled, her words not always too clear and mixed up
it is moments like these that set a mum's heart afire
so special, each and every one a jewel to forever treasure.
To watch her sleeping, her brow furled in sleep
little twitches as she dreams, her legs running
seeing her turn up her nose as cautiously she tastes
then spoons it down with a delighted smile that I return.
"Park, Mummy, park", she demands running to the door
standing there waiting impatiently as I put on her coat
holding hands, she skips alongside me giving the odd tug
running round playing on swings and seesawing with her friend
It is the small things in life that give most pleasure
and what is more enchanting than seeing your child have fun
watching them growing up exploring their small worlds
safe in the knowledge you are near as they stretch their horizons

Shadow Hamilton

Fishy Tale

A pond sits in the glen
bright fish dashing about
casting silvery shadows
ducks chasing after them
eels making their way to sea
flying birds circling back and forth
green frogs croaking for a mate
herons gobbling them up
in the depths a pike floats
jutting out its pointed head
keeping hidden as it prowls
lurking between the rotting logs
minnows swim by unharmed in shoals
newts eagerly snapping them up
out in the reeds lays up a catfish
playing dead, it patiently waits
quick to react to its prey
reaping the bounties little fry snack
sticklebacks swim lazily through reed beds
trout leaping catching fly's and midgets
under the calm waters life abounds
vivid rainbow trout spawn
while the blue waters thrive
xanthine filled plants floating
yellowfin cutthroat trout dart by and
zander perch fill a fisherman's net

Nature Visions

Relentless Time

As time ticks by relentlessly
we look back and wonder
where the hours and days have gone
they seem to have passed in a blink
When young we squander time
not yet understanding it's value
the years stretch out endless
we think nothing of yesterday
Yet as we age it seems to fly
now we take note and savour
each precious second, each memory
filling the pages of life
Age comes to all with the aches and pains
now we can relax and enjoy the hot sun
take time to enjoy simplicity
hoping for it to slow to our pace
But those seconds tick on relentless
time marches on regardless
have we filled the pages wisely?
as it comes time to pass on.

Shadow Hamilton

Danger Lurks

Danger lurks around every bend
as one travels the leafy path
peril in each step now does pend
With every move we must contend
as nature rages with her wrath
danger lurks around every bend
Passing onward through life we fend
with the odd brush we fight off death
peril in each step now does pend
Trouble everywhere we contend
pushing we travel every path
danger lurks around every bend
Battling our way through we vend
no time to stop and take a bath
peril in each step now does pend
Sometimes peace found in aftermath
as we outwit the psychopath
danger lurks around every bend
peril in each step now does pend

Nature Visions

Animals Alive

Gambit
Gambit you were such a friend
twenty years we had together
filled with the fun of your antics
like the time as a kitten
you jumped on the table
and sniffed a burning candle
you leapt up high and sideways
in shock and nasty surprise
every hair of your body on end
You hated it when I sang
and would get in my face
I knew if I did not stop
you would bite my nose
just like you did Rita's
one time when she was crying
which only made her howl the more
you ran our lives with military precision
food on the table right on time
or you would let us know you were not pleased
The black scourge of the neighbourhood
you intensely disliked the other cats
but also you hated it if you were alone
a special bond you shared with my dogs
to them you were always kind once they
knew their place that is, too boisterous
and your claws would inflict a scratch
as for the birds you hunted them with glee
often taking them out of the air as by they flew
Our twenty years together were not enough
I still miss you and your own lovable ways
Gambit dearest Gambit you were and are the best
unique and a tyrant you ruled my heart
fearless and bold you now await me in paradise

written 17 July 2014

Shadow Hamilton

Silver Beams

silver beams dancing
gently casting deep shadows
that seduce senses
icy waters plunge
steeply down into the lake
forming long ripples

Nature Visions

Reaffirmed

The leaves on the silver birch flutter
in the gentle breeze first silver then green
all around the fruit trees slowly growing
heavy as fruits swell and start to ripen
The flower buds break open in glorious colour
white scented flowers of mock orange rife
honey blossom cascading down walls
while sweet peas climb ever higher
Summer hot and sultry shows her face
to the earth's stunning painted canvas
and life once more renewed and vital
as all around us everything flourishes

Shadow Hamilton

Carelessness

A small pile of bone dry leaves lay
nestled, protected between two roots
It was a scorchingly hot sunny day
all the trees desperately needed rain
The land that had been without water
for so long was parched, all around
saplings drooping, dying for its lack
dust freely blowing, coating everything
The couple strolling, locked together
arm in arm, paused to admire the view
then settled on a fallen log, huddled
as they smoked, chatted and then kissed
The man pulled her up into his arms
carrying her further down the path
thoughtlessly chucking his lit cigarette
which landed on the small pile of leaves
Slowly the pile started to smoulder
wisps of smoke curling up in the air
a gentle breeze playfully fans them
small flames start to lick and spread
It hungrily consumes the plenteous fuel
first one tree then yet another it lights
soon the woods are blazing with its fury
it leaps from tree to tree, rapidly spreading
Catching the couple by surprise it devours them
and passes on, fiercely burning all in its path
by now firemen are fighting the advancing flames
struggling to douse it or bring it into control
Not succeeding, it has too firm a grip
raging it grows ever more gigantic
acres left scorched in its wake
carcasses litter the blacken land

Nature Visions

All seems to be totally lost, when
caring mother nature takes a hand
the wind swivels round creating a retreat
and so, slowly the fire dies of starvation

Shadow Hamilton

How Doth

How doth your face light up my life
with your winning winsome smile?
How doth your fair hair set me afire
as it blows carelessly in the breeze?
How doth your touch make me quiver
as you stroke with gentle hands?
How doth you thrill my every sense
as you collect me up into your arms?
How doth your strong limbs hold me
in closeness that enthrals my heart.
how doth just the sight of you
make me know that you love me?

Nature Visions

Goethe's Path

The forest path meandered through the trees
ahead the silvery tinkling sound of water
there was also a murmuring drone of bees
slowly slithering away was a sleepy adder
Entering the pretty glade full of flowers
his senses lulled by the peacefulness
watching with joy the diving dippers
and a kingfisher preening its feathers
Onward through the leafy forest he strolled
over on the right there were many fissures
as breathing heavily, he climbed up the wold
arriving at the huts of the wood dwellers
The high priest Druid Fire Dancer strode out
shouting welcome, come sit here by the fire
there roasting over the fire pit were trout
people dancing to the sweet tunes of the lyre

written 30 June 2014

Shadow Hamilton

Outback Truckers

Wheels turning, churning, fighting for a grip
mud oozing, clinging, sucking for purchase
rivers flooding their banks, water everywhere
trucks fighting trying to get through and deliver
their precious cargos that are desperately awaited
sometimes gasoline or much needed machinery
all depending on the driver to make it to them.
Rugged terrain scorching hot, dust billowing
rushing, rushing, thrusting ever onwards
on the lookout for wandering kangaroo's
hitting one can mean break down or overturning
tyres overheating and engines grumbling
break down out here and you are on your own
stranded until you fix the problem some how.
Massive extra wide loads, pain to get secure
permits needed before you can travel
limited to journeying only by night
desperately trying to make pull in spot
millions worth of cargo on board
and still three hundred and sixty kilometres
away from where you need to be.
Outriders ahead telling you when it is safe
to overtake that slow double trailer load
all hell breaking loose if they tell you wrong
stopping for pit stop and them going by
might be a hundred kilometres before
you can safely pass them once more
narrow or low bridges to navigate.
Will you ever get through before the Wet
closes everything down for months on end
risking the short cut praying it stays dry
if you are wrong stranded wheel deep in mud
tractors trying to pull you out, chains snapping

Nature Visions

digging frantically in terrible heat keeping eyes open
for them dratted snakes, at last you are free
Moving on only to get bogged down once more
and the whole process starts all over again
at last free and moving rapidly along
the load must get through at all costs
getting lost in the outback no fun
as you search for a place to safely turn
at last, reaching where you are supposed to be.
Dropping off lifesaving supplies and fuel
you reload and set off to do it all again
having to stop and re secure loose chains
three blowouts to fix, pray you have no more
you have used up all your spare tyres
brakes ceasing overheating you grind to a stop
sun blazing down as you fight to free them.
All these perils and many more are your woes
reputations on the line if you fail to deliver
so you drive on trying to make up lost time
family waiting, weeks since you last made it home
one last load to go before the Wet halts all
reaching your destination at long last
finally turning for the welcome journey home.

written 26 June 2014

Shadow Hamilton

Past Lives

I believe that in another life
a famous singer was what I had been
learning no voice I had gave me strife
this became apparent in my early teen
The flat out of tune caterwauling
instead of sweet pure notes
had both me and family cringing
only my lover on me singing dotes
I shed many tears as I needed to sing
my talking voice is dulcet like honey
in despair I tried to find something
poetry fills the gap with verses lovely
Now when I walk out onto the stage
I spin words that soar out like notes
as musical tunes in stories I now wage
my voice fills the room and music floats

written 24 June 2014

Uncle Roy

Uncle Roy written by Shadow Hamilton
As the evening drew in and birds settled to roost
the world seemed to give a collected sigh
as it stood poised waiting in the wings
the time had now come to gather up a soul
For a long time he had fought the invertible
reluctant to the end to leave and travel on
memories flashed past his eyes like a cine film
as a child playing with his siblings teasing Joyce
Play fighting with John rolling together over and over
learning the lessons of life and then a trade
meeting his Irish lassie so bonny, building a life
grieving together when children failed to join them
An upright man of principles that he held dear to his heart
Roy built a good life for himself and his Irish lassie Ann
standing strong for her when she was ill with tuberculosis
nursing her back to health passing his strength on to her
Wisely investing in his company shares they were never in need
were able to retire to the country for a new style of life
making many friends in their small village and just enjoying
their twilight years together with their two cats
Finally, he had to leave to travel beyond the veil
today we attend his funeral trying to make sense
of why he was snatched when life was so good
in each of his family's heart he will live on
His epitaph written deep in our souls
as we say our sad and lonely goodbyes
yet it is not the end as he still lives
deep within the hearts of all who love him

17 June 2014

Shadow Hamilton

Noble Beasts

The horse is a fascinating creature that serves us so well
Having had a life long relationship with horses
I am full of admiration for their endless toils.
They are fiery yet mainly gentle giants
and give hours of pleasure to their carers
I worked first as a working pupil
then in racing yards some flat but mainly jumping yards
going on to having my own stables
doing the show jumping circuit and some taming
I prefer the term taming to breaking in
it is all a matter of trust after all
why break a spirit? When with love
you get an unbreakable bond
Using this method I was able to school a horse
from wild to saddle in 2 to 3 weeks
then the real fun begins as you start
the real relationship of bringing it on
I had two people who taught me so much
when I was around 14 years old
we used to go in school holidays to the new forest
I told Maddie I wanted to become a show jumper
Now I was tiny about 4-foot 3 high
and she put me up on Yanta
he was 17 hands and a cat jumper
boy I had some spills over fences
Maddie's response was to take away my saddle
she said I needed to improve my seat and balance
well after many more spills it started working
and I became a burr on his back in total harmony
Later at 18 I started my training as a working pupil
training to be an instructor
now Heather was a tough cookie with quality horses
a formidable lady who took no excuses

She used to get us in the indoor school
taught us dressage and much more
some days she would remove both saddle and bridle
saying that a true rider steers with hands, knees and bodies
You riders try it sometime once you can back up a horse
and do flying changes and shoulder ins and outs
without any tackle then you are a rider
at one with your horse in body and soul
One of my pleasures has always been night riding
the horse is a prey animal and prone to flight
they get up on their toes and spook at shadows
riding without a saddle means you can feel each muscle tense
getting a sense of when they are ready to whirl and flee
leaving the unwary rider on the ground eating dust.
These two ladies shaped my life with horses
giving me insight into them and their needs
a sense of wonder and awe at their trust
and their willingness to work with us
Be they an Arab or thoroughbred or plain Jane
each one teaches us so much as we interact
there is nothing more heart warming than
a horse nickering to you delighted you are there
shaking and tossing their heads stamping the ground
impatient for you to stroke and caress them
giving you comfort when you are down
and joy when you are up and excited
Now no longer able to ride due to a bad hip
I still share a close bond and delight
when I call to horses in a field
and they come at a charge to greet me
it is the simple things that give the most pleasure

Shadow Hamilton

I Did It My Way

I often do things my way
sometimes getting into trouble
especially when I was younger
the rules were there for breaking
A real scourge when at school
my teachers often despaired
boarding school was not fun
except for secret midnight rides
Even now I still go my way
although staying within the law
my dad says I have my own way
of doing things, he is quite right
I just refuse to be a sheep
blindly following the others
if it does not make sense
then I always go my own way
footnote
I used to sneak out on moonlit nights catch up a horse and ride it through the fields
with just a halter or bridle great fun

Nature Visions

Lonely Cloud

A lonely cloud sat on a mountain
looking for someone to play with
staring out over landscape
he saw friends far away
with a puff he flew
to join with them
they had fun
playing
ball

written 31 May 2014

Shadow Hamilton

All About Leadership

I come to you with love in my heart
in you I place all my trust
joining you in your nature walks
lying close by your side at night
I sense your tension and panic
and stand guarding you from danger
for you I would give my very life
I cower not understanding your anger
As you shout at me I cringe at your feet
all I want to do is to love and protect you
now as we walk you are so tense
so once more you I protect
Confused when you jerk me back
and scold me for I know not what
then a calm man appears and explains
it is not me but you, I just need a pack leader
Cesar shows you how to step up
to be calm yet assertive
love alone he explains is not enough
no dog is born bad I just needed guidance
Now when we go out for walks
I now bound along happily
the tension that was is gone
thanks to that wise calm man
a tribute to Cesar Millan and the work he does

Moonlight Passion

Taking a blanket they headed for their favourite spot
a secluded place in a glade beside the gurgling river
this haven was filled with the scent of damask roses
and sweet honeysuckle grew rampantly up the trees
Laying the fleecy blanket on the soft grassy ground
sank down into each other's arms with gentle sighs
the moonlight was filtering down between the trees
lending a sense of romance, oh how they loved it here
Slowly. softly they began to caress gently stirring passions
their exuberant loving sighs carrying in the still night airs
afterwards they would lie spoon shaped, sated by love
then slowly they gathered up their blanket with a last kiss
Time now to return to their every day life's of the mundane
treasuring these stolen hours that added most romantic spice
after twenty five years of marriage and raising five children
it was these precious moments that renewed their love

Shadow Hamilton

Elephant Rage. A True Story

Harry was waiting at base camp for his party of tourists
hoping that Beverly and her children would not be rowdy.
When they finally arrived, he got them settled in their tent.
Once unpacked they joined him in the main area for tea.
After he had explained the rules they chatted about this and that.
Her children Ben and Sue were lively but very well behaved.
Harry promised to take them on a safari the very next day,
he said there was a waterhole a few miles away from camp.
As they sat there finishing off their tea Samari ran into camp
he said less than a mile away there was a solitary elephant.
So they made their way carefully to where he was last seen,
he had moved on into the thick bush they cautiously followed.
After five hundred yards or more they could hear him nearby,
suddenly the elephant screamed and charged at them.
They all ran as fast as they could the ground shaking under their feet
his trumpeting roars were deafening as quickly he caught up.
Then Beverly and the children reached the open plains,
Samari was with them and they sighed in relief at escaping.
This relief was short lived when they realised Harry was missing
the elephant had picked him out to follow and was gaining fast.
Harry could feel him closing its breath blowing on his neck
desperately he zigzagged trying to lose it to little avail.
He looking back could see the bristles of it's trunk hairs
then it struck him with its trunk knocking him to the floor.
Harry rolled up into a ball and lay still as possible playing dead.
The elephant kicked him around like a ball then caught him up
and flung him in the air as Harry landed, he pointed trying to scare it,
upon which the elephant gored his leg with a tusk then walked away.
Harry was bleeding badly he tried hard to stop the blood flow,
he could see it pumping out at an alarming rate, he knew he needed help.
Meantime Beverly and Samari were carefully searching for him
at last Samari heard his weak whimpers and tracked him down.
Quickly he tore off his shirt and bound it tightly round the leg

Nature Visions

managing to slow the blood to a trickle he radioed for help.
Harry was fading in and of consciousness as Beverly cradled his head
at last the Jeep arrived and he was taken to a plane and flown to hospital.
Once there they operated and sewed him up, he needed six pints of blood,
he thought of his mother realising he never said goodbye to her.
Slowly he recovered back in England and told his mum he was sorry
that in his excitement he had forgotten she immediately forgave him.
When he was fit again, he decided to return to Africa once more
to face his fears head on as he had loved his time on the dark continent.
He knew this was not the time to cower away letting his fears rule
so boldly he took his courage in both hands and flew back to base.
After all the measure of a person is to always face and live life
and it was he and his party who had trespassed in the elephant's land.
A lesson well learned from then on he always carried a gun,
not to hunt with, but to protect the tourists who came to see the game.

Shadow Hamilton

School Gate

The day began like every other day
no hint of what was to happen
taking the children to school
she saw a man near the gates
He smiled at her and tipped his cap
tall and handsome around her age
sadly when she came out he was gone
with a sign she walked on to work
The sun was blazing down baking all
so she took her sandwich outside
sitting at a bench in the local park
she espied him running in the distance
His long legs eating up the ground
he soon disappeared from sight
longing to meet and talk to him
she sat there as long as she dared
Reluctantly returning to work
day dreaming about him passed the time
at last it was time to collect the kids
again, he was waiting as they came out
She noticed him with two children
but when she turned right he went left
wondering why she had not seen him before
sad that he seemed happily married
For the next few days she kept seeing him
mainly he was far off in the distance
Until one day arriving early at the gates
she saw him waiting there for his kids
Shyly she stood nearby giving him a smile
he walked over and started to chat
she soon learned they were his nieces
and he was helping his sister
His sister's husband was away fighting

Nature Visions

and was deployed in the middle east
as he was between jobs and she pregnant
he helped by taking the girls to school
Slowly their feelings turned to love
she had lost her husband to war in Iran
and he had lost his wife to cancer two years ago
against the odds once more they both found love

written 17 May 2014

Shadow Hamilton

Day the Earth Reversed

In the blink of an eye the earth reversed
the sun rising in the west setting in the east
gravity's pull suddenly lessened it's hold
heavy things grow much lighter and floated
Look up to the sky and see what I mean
houses, cars animals and people flying
water running uphill instead of down
mighty oceans now the sky adorn
All still just kept within earth's strati-fear
beneath shines a land so strange
empty lakes and ponds now up in the sky
bewildered animals flying by, oh so high
As the day grew slowly to its close
gravity started to righten herself
and things began to resettle themselves
yet landing in totally different places
The poles became hot lands of sunshine
while the tropics were buried deep in snow
oh what a pickle it all was the army striving
to return things to normal but all in vain
Mammoth rescues of creatures to their normal climes
speed was all important before they perished
to our credit most were rescued and re-homed
our earth always mysterious is now reversed
How will we cope in these new places
well come back in a thousand years
I suspect human nature will be unchanged
still the same old BS run by the same morons

Swimming With Dolphins

When my daughter was fifteen
we went on holiday to Cyprus
always a life long desire of hers
was to swim with a dolphin
Imagine her delight and joy
when we saw a sign for this
paying for her was not cheap
but maybe the best sum ever spent
At the pool we watched the display
then off she went to kit up
on returning she was first
boy he sure took her for a ride
When she returned poolside
that dolphin kept returning to her
though others were waiting their turn
the delight on her face spoke volumes
At the end we all got to stroke it
and wow I have never felt so good
its skin was like nothing I have ever touched
silky smooth magical feel, a memory that lives on
I even got a dolphin's kiss
as I knelt beside it

Shadow Hamilton

In the Gloaming

The hunter set off just before the gloaming
adjusting the straps of his high powered rifle
it was a long way to where the stag usually fed
a majestic stag sprouting twelve point antlers
Climbing high up the rugged mountain side
he trekked fast covering the many miles
at last he was where the stag usually fed
casting around for signs of his tracks
Finding them he started stalking his prey
uphill and down dale he carefully followed
until at last he could see him way up ahead
taking care to keep down wind he got close
Now about one hundred yards apart, he settled
nestling into the thick bracken patiently waiting
The stag climbed onto his favourite outlook
and stood there poised as the gloaming lit the sky
Truly a wondrous sight he was in full prime
the hunter sighed as he took steady aim
then with a click it was finally time to shoot
the stag hearing the sound took to his heels
The hunted checked his camera, yes he had him
a perfect picture well satisfied he packed up
this one picture had taken days of trailing him
now he was forever captured in magnificent splendour

Nature Visions

Ode To My Hills

Driving home, the sun beaming down
highlighting the Quantock foothills
a criss-cross quilt of very small fields
too steep for mechanical ploughs
worked still by man and shire horses
Bright gleaming yellow rape and mustard
interwoven with shades of brilliant green
a paradise for birds nesting in the hedges
tiny dots of white sheep scattered round
deep scarlet red of the fields laid to fallow
Ancient hills stun with captivating beauty
hardwood trees hundreds of years old
spread their sheltering branches wide
casting fat and long shadows "neath their feet
grassy banks giving shelter to small animals
I gaze with delight filling up my soul
loving the fact these are my hills
that roll and soar around my village
with magical names for each hill
some very bare others full of heather
Reminding me of my native home
Will's Neck and Cothelstone
rearing up above the deep valleys
with nestling lakes and rivers
this place my place till I pass on
these hills were the first place in England to be given the title of outstanding beauty

1956 check them out in Wikipedia for these amazing views

Shadow Hamilton

Moon Ode

Moon you serenade me nightly
casting your beaming silvery rays
touching and filling my weary soul
with awesome magical perfection
Watching you in your various phases
crescent sliver you delight and enchant
yet too your half sends heartfelt shivers
as you wax your way to full glowing light
moon dear moon you rule my senses
as you wane, the sea's tides join you
making my moods shift with your cycles
your whims commanding earth herself
I serenade and worship your beauty
disliking intensely nights you are cloaked
when clouds hid you from earthly sight
then with a peek you emerge triumphant
And now once more my heart rejoices

written 8. May 2014

As Darkness Descends

As the sun slowly sets beneath the horizon
the world starts to turn to night's darkness
the shadows gradually lengthen then fade
and a stillness covers the land with mystery
This is the time for the creatures of night
the badgers sniff the air before leaving their sett
then come tumbling out to play in moonlit glade
while the adults set of to do their foraging
The wise owls sit in tall trees their heads twisting
as they filter the sounds of small rustles and squeaks
then do, on silent wings glide and hit with deadly strike
carrying their offerings back to their hungry fledglings
The wolf sets off on his nightly quest hunting for prey
if the moon is full he will climb up high and sing to it
then just a grey shadow as through the undergrowth
he slips, then belly down as he creeps closer and kills
Now it is time for other less salubrious creatures
the ones that haunt our dreams and disturb our sleep
for unmentionable things to walk the night time trails
now is their time to catch an unwary soul who lingered
Secrets hidden in the dark a grave or two lie unmarked
a deadly silence now hangs and people scuttle home
tuck themselves up safe indoors to await the sun's return
the darkness fades and the sun once more comes out to play

Shadow Hamilton

The Darkness At Noon

As the moon passes over the sun
the earth to darkness is plunged
in olden times people were in fear
thinking this is the world's end
Pitch blackness covers the earth
day and night are now reversed
no bird songs now can be heard
just an ominously deep silence
slowly so slowly the light returns
a collective sigh of relief from all
today is not yet the world's end
just an eclipse of startling magnitude

7 May 2014

Nature Visions

Silent Killer

It courses through the blood
hidden from view it seeks out
the T-cells attaching itself
it silently goes to work
Invading and taking over
not caring if it's host
be a young person or old
killing of the white cells
Your gender it cares nothing for
or if you are straight or gay
insidiously it can hide for years
a master of disguise it patiently waits
Growing stronger all the time
breaking down the body's defences
it corrupts turning cells alien
not caring that as it slowly kills
That eventually it will too die
that as it completes its invasion
leaving a sick body open to attack
covered with open sores and abrasions
This silent killer in murdering you
does itself meet its own doom
dying along with its host
will we ever find a real cure?
This is about Aids/ HIV though it could also refer to cancer HIV is ingenious in
its ability to hide itself inspires by Harlan Coben's book Miracle cure

Shadow Hamilton

Gender Bender

On getting up I looked in the mirror
and to my amazement I saw I was a man
what fun I thought lets have some fun
I dressed in a man's suit and went to work
Driving there in my new Porsche
I gave the pretty girls a wave
I got lots of smiles and a few winks
laughing I arrived at the office
Getting a fair few back slaps
as the guys drooled over my wheels
some winks and nudges, suggestive remarks
Hey Joe, who's your lucky date tonight?
With this machine the worlds your oyster
listening to their bawdy jokes I hide a smile
And relish the tall tales of their own conquests
so this is what goes on in the men's room
How they would cringe faces red if they knew
that no man was I just a lass who awoke a man
driving home my husband was cooking that night
dressed up to the nines in my best black dress
I had to laugh as he tottered on my stiletto heels
boy did he made a nice woman wearing a long wig
the food he made was no great shakes just uggy
but the love making more than made up for it
Next morning I approached the mirror
and soon saw that I was back to normal
Joe looked at me and grinned in delight
He said I made a better man than him
But we had better keep it quiet
as his co-workers would not live it down
I enjoyed my day as a man very much
seeing life from the other side

written 4 May 2014

Nature Visions

Viking Plunder

The Viking gallery slipped quietly through the night
the oars just barely skimming the gentle swell
sails were furlowed tight to help hide it from sight
the warriors ready for the signal sounded by the bell
Silently they landed, ferocious was their appearance
wielding their great battle axes wearing winged helmets
they crept up on the sleeping village in timeless trance
plundering and pillaging killing some helpless pets
Taking captive the fairest of the maids enslaving burly men
to work the gallery's oars, filling the hold with stolen treasure
drinking wine from carved horns and spit roasting a tasty hen
soon well into their cups they ravished most maids keeping one pure
She of flaxen hair and hour glass figure and tender years was spared
a most fitting present for their king, the rest would be auctioned for profit
the coin added to the treasury. Now under full sail the waves they dared
knowing a welcome most raucous awaited they now their torches lit
Their king was most pleased with his gift and vowed they would be wed
a great feast was prepared and the mead flowed thick and sweetly
the Viking cheered as their king took the maid first as wife then to bed
weeping as she was ravished, he rode her like a bull until she bled badly
Back to the feast he downed some horns then lay down to sleep
the maid waited until all was silent and then into his heart she struck deep
she took back her shame as he lay dying knowing her own death she did reap
turning the dagger on herself her life no value she slipped into eternal sleep

written 1 May 2014

Shadow Hamilton

Old Loves

Many the people I have known
a few who were once loved with hot passion,
most insubstantial shadows lost in time
a few remembered well and most fondly.
As for me, am I remembered too?
If so, with fondness left lingering?
or by other less salubrious thoughts?
Where did they end up these ghosts of mine?
Some, just a brief fling, then on
to pastures not always any greener
with the same everyday strife's
that tear and weaken the fabric.
Love always arrives most joyously
fanfare heralds it in the door
Yet just as fast it flees in the dark
Leaving the remnants behind to pick over
To truly love is a perfect gift
granted only to a precious few
empowering them as it laps over them
so I say to long ago loves, Be Happy

Nature Visions

Flower Garden

Asters litter beds in rainbow colours
Berries red and black slowly growing
Clover adding bright patches of green
Daisy's dotting the rolling lawns
Enchanting us with their beauty
Fox gloves waving their wands of trumpets
Gerbera brightly show the sun their faces
Hibiscus blown by gentle hot breezes sway
Irises joining in glinting and glimmering
Jasmine flowers spreading out profusely as
Kale fish swim in the pond flashing colour
Lilies floating gracefully give them shelter
Mums giving ground cover to the rolling banks with
Narcissus poking out between them while the
Orange hues of asters are a delightful background for
Peonies some tall most very short nestle beneath
Quince flowers, still their tight buds vie with
Roses stately and wafting perfume clouds around
Snapdragons closing their petals over insects
Tansy's rarely seen now a days, here do thrive and
Uniformly line the garden paths whilst timid
Violets of deep purple shyly peek out and the
White tulips dance amid the rest under hedges of
Xylosma giving height and deep shade for plants
Zinnia's with rings of colour exploding

24 April 2014

Shadow Hamilton

Secrets

She was wearing a mask
silver it glints in light
soon it will be removed
silence now fills the room
slowly all revealed
some then are compromised
Secrets now all do see

26 April 2014

Nature Visions

A Daydream

She stares lost, into the distance
far removed from the sounds of life.
Her book, she ignores, as she ponders
soft are her eyes as memories surface.
She starts as her hand hits the keys
then plays a few notes in remembrance.
Mundanely trying to fill up her time
she waits, watching, her mind still lost.
Her heart is yearning for his presence
without him, she feels, oh so incomplete.
Soon now he should be returning home
she prays he will share her joyful news.
A small flutter inside her womb
signifies the start of new life.
Will he be happy or angry with her,
although this birth was not planned.
She knows he wanted to wait a bit
get a promotion or two at his work.
Yet the fates have decreed otherwise.
She hears the door and his footsteps.
He calls out her name as he enters
and pulls her into a loving embrace.
She stiffens in his arms, feeling scared,
then stammers to him, her life changing news
He goes as still as death itself, shocked,
walks away from her to pour a stiff drink.
Then suddenly it hits him, they will be parents,
joyfully he holds her, asking when in excitement.
About seven months time she softly whispers.
Her joy set alight with love for him and her unborn child.
A boy, she hopes, just like his handsome father
and they celebrate together their happiness.

written 26 April 2014

Shadow Hamilton

For the Love Of

Love comes in many forms
is covered by many guises
sacrifices made are many
just for its glorious name
I have many loves in life
the love of early morning
as the sun peeks out
slowly rising to its zenith
Or the breeze rustling
stirring up the leaves
as if a sprite is hiding
and is shaking them
The moon with majesty
lighting our path
as it shines beaming
casting its silvery light
To be up high looking
out over the landscape
the patchwork fields
and small dots of cattle
The sheer beauty of the waterfall
as it cascades down laughing in joy
to join the lake sparkling bright
love of the startling beauty it creates
For the simple joy of just being alive
with people you love by your side
supporting you when they are needed
staunchly standing in your corner
For the love of oh so much
joy in everyday things
always being open
ready for new adventures

Nature Visions

These things and so many more
are what makes life interesting
excitement over what is over the brow
of the love of each new challenge

Shadow Hamilton

Do You Really Know Him

She fell in love with him and they married
soon after the first child was born a girl
he never seemed to forge a link with her
never really created that magical bond
Later she would look back and see
all that she had been blind about
now could clearly see the cracks
how had she ever missed them?
Always a rather secretive man
never letting people get close
he would take to the open road
calling on clients making sales
Far and wide he did travel
but never seemed to get ahead
losing job after job he would rail
cursing his luck blaming others
One day she got very suspicious
noticing the stories online
of women disappearing without trace
others raped and murdered
She felt shivers of fear could it be?
checking the areas where he worked
seeing a pattern begin to emerge
she called the sheriff's office
They soon dropped by plus FBI
and after questioning her
searched down in their basement
finding there all sorts of proof
Trophies he had taken and kept
purses, bits of jewellery and hair
Jar containing horror full of fingers
in a couple there were eyeballs

Nature Visions

She had lived with this monster
slept together never realising
their daughter now was fifteen
and prone to strange silences
They watched together as
he was caught and led away
no tears fell from either of them
she caught up in all the horror
Could only look at her daughter
and wonder, yes wonder
did the apple fall close to the tree?
was she also tainted like him?
With her weird silences that shut her out
the neighbourhood pets found tortured
a sense of fear when she was behind you
the blood sometimes on her clothes
In the end fearful for her own life
she had her committed to bedlam
her daughter capable and willing
another killer now locked away

Newness of Life
In Spring young thoughts turn to fancy
life around us is renewed
ladies wearing gowns all chintzy
Do entice men with a curtsey
careful least it's a wedding bed
in Spring young thoughts turn to fancy
Now the ladies, a few doxy's
love to spin, their skirts all spread
Ladies wearing gowns all chintzy
Love comes courting in ecstasy
the fashion this year is redheads
in Spring young thoughts turn to fancy
The ladies are so full of moxie
lead men on but no maidenhead
ladies wearing gowns all chintzy

Shadow Hamilton

Fluttering eyelids so saucy
men their passions this time unfed
in Spring young thoughts turn to fancy
ladies wearing gowns all chintzy

Nature Visions

A Broken Heart

A most strange creature walked into the room
upright on two legs he stood oh so very tall
dressed in fine array booted and suited
a hat perched jauntily on his head
He cast around the room eyeing people up
as he strutted back and forth leaving in his wake
a deep silence of disbelief as the folks all stared
and started to draw back as they saw his tail
Not a person was this uninvited guest
no even though dressed as a man
he was a ferocious gorilla in love
seeking out his Jane he hunted around
Not finding her he stood confused
gaping at the people in their finery
come on now said his keeper catching up
and he led him back to his cage
The gorilla sits there tear running down his face
lost without his Jane he sits in desolation
she had passed away only 5 months ago
now he hunts for her whenever he can
His keeper has tried to jolly him along
even introducing a young lady or two
met with indifferent then ignored
he only wants his true love Jane

Shadow Hamilton

Ghost Rider

When the moon is new and casting little light
as the wind whispers through the leafy trees
and millions of tiny pin prick stars light the sky
this is the time you will hear hooves on the breeze
The ghost rider follows the trails ever searching
no fearsome ghost this, just a poor sad lost soul
ever hunting for his lady who's life was cut short
snatched from him in fullness of life by illness
He haunts the places they used to walk together
no peace or rest for him when the moon is new
his steed once fiery now plods tired of the journey
tied together to this mortal coil of loss and regret
Yet each spring solstice together they are seen
their horses galloping towards one another
and once more they ride and stroll the paths
lovers now again reunited in joyful passion

Nature Visions

Lost

The small band of travellers struggled on
they had been lost for days in the dunes
driven nearly mad by thirst and heat
and flickering mirages of fresh cool water
Pangs of hunger long gone in their need
for even a single gulp of life saving water
at last reaching the top of the sand dune
they rubbed their eyes and looked again
Yes, it really was an oasis not a dream
tumbling down the dune in their haste
at last they reached the small pool
carefully they took a few sips then more
Knowing how close it had been
they rejoiced and gave thanks
soon a fine settlement appeared
and the travellers prospered there
They had fought through their ordeal
learned that life is unpredictable
yet with each other they conquered
and found new hope and new meaning

Shadow Hamilton

The Drifter

Now Jack was a man who had seen much
as an army brat he travelled the world
never really making friends at each stop
he slipped into the role of soldier
Soon was made up to major in the Mps
betrayed by his superiors he began to drift
moving from town to town, just a backpack
to his name doing odd jobs here and there
Trouble seemed to find him where ever he was
always ready to help the underdog sort problems
living under the blanket using president's names
foot loose and certainly fancy free with no ties
Looking for him is like looking for a ghost
your best chance is a message left at his bank
and maybe if he is intrigued enough, he may
just look you up and sort out your strife
One thing you should know for sure
is one morning he will be gone on his way
the vista of the blue unknown calling
for now Jack drifts along life's highways

Nature Visions

The Stones

The stones quivered,
pulsing in her hands
their beauty enthralling.

written 12 April 2014

Shadow Hamilton

Life's Mountain

One climbs the mountain of life
some full of hope others with fear
each one taking a separate path
already making life changing choices
For some the climb long and arduous
with glimpses of hope and happiness
most trudge along going both up and down
never reaching their true potential
For a rare few plain sailing awaits their hopes
do these give back or help those who struggle?
For them who conquer their personal Everest
satisfaction their time here was so well spent

Nature Visions

Hitching a Ride

Going deep into the valley as the last rays fade
in the big clearing there waiting for me is Snowflake
now he is a Unicorn that kindly takes me on journeys
to wondrous far off mystical realms that astound
Climbing onto his back we set off at speed of light
soaring high we circled the moon saying how do you do
to the blue cheese man who doffs his hat and bows
then sends beams of bright rays to lighten our path
Then racing a shooting star leaving it far behind
onward to Saturn where we dance through its rings
leaving the best to last, we fly on to the lady herself
Venus the enchantress, the planet of love that enthrals
Filled to the brim with the sights and the wonder
we drift down to land hugging Snowflake who wickers
then flies off into the dawn fast becoming a disappearing dot
leaving me to wander homeward drinking in creations miracles

written 04/04/2014

Shadow Hamilton

A Ring of Stones

You sit majestically sometimes dark and brooding
other times flooded with light you seem to glow
towering high over all you survey standing sentry
you dominate the landscape for many miles.
Used for many rituals maybe also some bloodshed
for centuries druids, wickers and more worship
at your feet each with their own purpose and dreams
the mystery you hold still not fully understood
It is said you can be seen from far away in space
that with others you form a ring around the earth
to walk through you touching your stones
gave me such a thrill (not allowed any more)
They say the acid on our hands damages you
so now you are fenced off so none can approach
the seance of you calls to me as I pass you by
may you Stonehenge be part of our heritage for ever

An Ode For Zante

I had not long lost Shona (German Shepherd) and was not sure because of my age and disabilities if I should get another when my daughter spotted an advert.
I thought long and hard and having always since the age of seven had my own dog
I decided that there were ways around my disability.
I went to the farm you were born on and met Matthew and your mum Lady.
Matthew suggested we met the 3 puppies left and take them down the fields so I could
choose. He let you all out and we started off by the time we reached the gate Lady and two pups had run on ahead. I looked at Matthew who had not noticed and said I have be chosen he looked in surprise and said so you have.
Needless to say I took you home and thus began a wonderful relationship you were highly intelligent I remember the first time you saw TV you were glued to the screen. We started obedience classes when you were 6 months old and soon you were in the top class. I quickly learnt when a new challenge or lesson was started to hang back and let you watch. Then when it was your turn you went out and did it nearly perfectly and always nailed it on your second attempt.
You had a yellow squeaky dog toy that you liked to live just outside the door and you would nuzzle it going in and out. One day my daughter said to me Zante thinks it her puppy doesn't she I said yes, then my daughter told me she had thrown it for her and that she went mental checking it was not hurt.
I knew you longed to be a mum so when you were two you went to a good dog and
in time produced nine fine puppies you were so happy and a wonderful mum.
I with your agreement moved yellow squeaky dog to the kitchen window sill.
When the day came for them to go as each one left you lay crying softly by the back

gate and I joined you shedding my own tears.

Two years later after some notable wins in the ring by you and your daughter

Tanganyika you again became a mum to 8 fine pups. Tanganyika did not understand

why you growled and sent her away. You finally allowed her to meet them at around

4 weeks. This time we kept two a dog and a b**ch, still we both cried when parting time came.

I did not know we were on borrowed time and that a year later at only six and half years you developed very aggressive cancer and faded in under 3 weeks I held you here at home while you tried to stand to say hello to the vet you could not get up,

the cancer had sapped your strength.

I cried buckets as we said goodbye and you slipped off to peace and heaven I buried you at home with your yellow squeaky dog that still squeaked and your

favourite blanket. There is an uncarved stone marking the spot in your favourite

corner of the garden.

I still miss you so much as does Tanganyika who went on the following spring on win 3rd at Cruft's 2010 you would have been so proud.

Zante you stole my heart and gave me a new leash on life You will always live

in my heart YOU WERE THE BEST 2003 -2009

Fisherman

The fisherman sat on the bank
patiently he waits for a bite
but his reel stayed very lank
He wanted to score a good rank
but was having no luck at this site
the fisherman sat on the bank
A few nibbles and his reel sank
his bait gone, words he did incite
but his reel stayed very lank
With a splash his reel it did tank
with a whooping enormous bite
the fisherman sat on the bank
The gods up above he did thank
his luck he believed not quite
but his reel stayed very lank
By now he had got very dank
and shaking off a pesky mite
the fisherman sat on the bank
but his reel stayed very lank

Shadow Hamilton

Poets of Yore

As I peruse the magnificent works of poets long gone
read their words of love, wisdom, pain and suffering
I am uplifted and filled with awe at what they achieved
all this without modern aids, most read after they are gone
I pause and think what would they produce if still alive
were able to get the instant feedback of modern times
could write their poems not on paper as in oldie days
able to use computers and easily store their precious works
Think of the realms of paper screwed up and tossed away
a start, an inkling of an idea that will not freely flow
how they sweated searching for a particular phrase
read, ponder and be amazed at their outstanding works
So raise your glass in a toast to their ingeniousness
Salute them for they fought hard to bring us joy
delighting hearts holding us in the palms of their hands
such power do they still wield over each of us modern poets

Nature Visions

The Magical Forest

Walk along the leafy paths dappled with shade
turn over a rock or two and watch the scurrying
as little insects scatter looking for some covering
finding it underneath some sticks and a grass blade
Sit quietly and just listen to the song birds singing
with music and beauty they fill the forest glade
then walk down to the gurgling stream and wade
cooling feet in its crystal water with lots of splashing
Turn over the leaf of a fern and see the spores clinging
watch the leaves waving in the breeze as they are frayed
then some red deer fawns bucked, frolicked and played
not seeming to care who was there, jumping and springing
Squirrels chattering angrily as they send nuts down in a cascade
bombarding all who pass by, they seem to lie, hidden and waiting
to catch unsuspecting walkers as they explore without disturbing
taking care to preserve the wafts of bluebells and deadly nightshade
Wandering onwards seeing the silky cocoon of a future butterfly cacheted
and mushroom rings surround the tall trees mystical and captivating
some plain, many with multi-coloured spots in sunshine glittering
old oak trees stand in splendour with leaves of emerald, turquoise and jade
Arriving at the banks of the lake surrounded by the forest glade
this place of mystery and tranquillity, no need of further searching
all one could ask for, spread out in glorious array that is so fitting
walking home I am content that into the magical forest today I strayed

written 03/13/2014

Printed and bound by CPI Group (UK) Ltd, Croydon, CR0 4YY